Jasper Warren is a [...] the tragedy that's marred his life. He's on a road to nowhere with his roommate, Lacy, whom he adores, and a dead-end retail job in Chicago.

And then everything changes in a single night. Though Jasper doesn't know it, his road *is* going somewhere after all. This time when tragedy strikes, it brings with it Lacy's older, wealthy, sexy uncle Rob. Despite the heart-wrenching circumstances, an immediate connection forms between the two men.

But the secrets between them test their attraction. Will their revelations destroy the bloom of new love... or encourage it to grow?

THE SECRETS WE KEEP

Rick R. Reed

A NineStar Press Publication

www.ninestarpress.com

The Secrets We Keep

Printed in the USA

Print ISBN: 978-1-64890-043-3

First Edition, July, 2020
Originally Published in September, 2019

Also available in eBook, ISBN: 978-1-64890-042-6

Warning: This book contains sexually explicit content,
which may only be suitable for mature readers, death of
a prominent character, suicide, and description of past
murder.

For Bruce...Again

I want to be with those who know secret things or else alone.
    —Rainer Maria Rilke

And when at last you find someone to whom you feel you can pour out your soul, you stop in shock at the words you utter—they are so rusty, so ugly, so meaningless and feeble from being kept in the small cramped dark inside you so long.
    —Sylvia Plath, *The Unabridged Journals of Sylvia Plath*

THE SECRETS WE

KEEP

Rick R. Reed

A NineStar Press Publication

www.ninestarpress.com

The Secrets We Keep

Printed in the USA

Print ISBN: 978-1-64890-043-3

First Edition, July, 2020
Originally Published in September, 2019

Also available in eBook, ISBN: 978-1-64890-042-6

For Bruce...Again

I want to be with those who know secret things or else alone.

     —Rainer Maria Rilke

And when at last you find someone to whom you feel you can pour out your soul, you stop in shock at the words you utter—they are so rusty, so ugly, so meaningless and feeble from being kept in the small cramped dark inside you so long.

     —Sylvia Plath, *The Unabridged Journals of Sylvia Plath*

Prologue

"Hey! I don't think you should go through that," Rob said, barely audible because he didn't want his fear to show. He sucked in a breath and clutched his suitcase close to him, as though it were a child—or a flotation device. Or a boy he loved and didn't want to lose...

The water spread out on the road under the overpass like a black mirror. It could have been a few inches deep or a few feet. From just a visual, there was no way to gauge how deep it was. No person with any sense would drive *into* it.

His Uber driver, a sallow-complexioned man in his forties wearing a black baseball cap, gave out a low whistle. "We'll be okay," he said cheerfully, with a confidence Rob simply didn't have. "Just sit back and let me worry. We'll be fine."

Rob wished he had the nerve to speak up, to command, "No! Don't! Just turn around." After all, this driver was putting them both in danger. But he felt like protesting would make him seem insane or, at the very least, silly. So what's worse, he wondered, seeming crazy or drowning? He cursed himself for the ridiculous lengths he went to so as to avoid confrontation.

A thunderclap as loud as an explosion sounded then, and Rob swore the black Lincoln Continental shuddered under its vibration. Lightning turned the dark, cloud-choked dawn skies bright white for an instant, as though day had peeked in, seen the weather, and then ducked back out.

"This baby can get through it," the driver said, giving the car a little more gas.

Rob tightened his lips to a single line and furrowed his brows as his driver set off into the small lake stretching out before them. As the driver moved completely under the overpass, the drumming sound of the rain on the roof suddenly ceased, and the silence was like the intake of a breath.

"C'mon, c'mon," the driver urged almost under his breath as he sallied farther into the water, giving the car more gas.

Even before the engine started to whine in protest, Rob knew they were in trouble by the way the water parted to admit the Lincoln. Waves sloshed by on either side.

Rob thought again he should speak up—like maybe to suggest that the driver could attempt to back up—but held his tongue. The guy was a professional, right? He knew what he was doing.

They'd be okay.

And the driver continued, deeper and deeper into the water standing so treacherously beneath the overpass.

The engine made a lowing sound, like a cow's moo, as the flood rose up the sides of the vehicle.

Rob gasped as brackish, foul-smelling water covered his loafered feet, pouring in through the small spaces around the doors.

The driver eyed him in the rearview mirror. There was a defeat in his voice as he said, "You better open your door and get out while you can."

Rob wondered, for only a moment, why he would want to. Then it struck him with the adrenaline-fueled clarity born of panic that if he didn't open his door now, he might never get another chance. The rising water and its pressure would make it impossible to open the door.

If it wasn't already too late...

Rob leaned over and pressed against the door. The engine stalled at that moment, and his driver reached for his own door handle up front.

For a brief moment that caused his heart to drum fast, Rob feared his door wouldn't open. He slid over and leaned against it with his shoulder pressed against the black leather, grunting.

The door held and then suddenly gave way.

Granted access, water rushed into the vehicle. The icy current rose up, covering his ankles and his calves. It was almost over his knees when he managed to slide from the Lincoln.

Outside the car, he stood. The water rose up almost to his neck. He felt nothing, only a kind of numbness and wonder. His driver was already sloshing forward toward the pearly light at the other side of the overpass. He didn't give Rob so much as a backward glance.

Rob started moving against the water, wondering what might be swimming in it.

Thunder grumbled and then cracked again. The lightning flared, brilliant white, once more. And the rain poured down even harder.

He looked back for a moment at the Lincoln Continental, thinking about his TUMI bag on the seat. There was no hope for that now!

He slogged through the water and progressed steadily forward, feeling like a refugee in some third-world country, bound for freedom. In his head he heard the swell of inspirational music.

After what seemed like an hour, but was really only about five minutes, Rob reached dry land at the end of the overpass, where the entrance ramp veered upward toward the highway. Cars whizzed by, sending up sprays of water, the motorists oblivious.

His driver eyed him but said nothing. He was out of breath.

Rob stood in the rain and remembered his iPhone in the front pocket of his khakis. He pulled it out, thinking to call for help. But when he pressed the Home button, the screen briefly illuminated and then blinked out, the picture of an ocean wave crashing toward the shore first skewing weirdly, then vanishing.

"Shit," he whispered and then replaced the phone in his soaking-wet pants pocket.

He needn't have worried about calling for help, however, because it seemed the universe had done it for him. On the other side of the overpass, a fire truck, lights on but no siren, pulled up to the water's edge. Then two police cruisers. And finally, surprisingly, a news van with a satellite antenna on top brought up the rear.

The rest was kind of a blur. Through a bullhorn, one of the firemen advised them to come back toward them but to use the median instead of slogging through the flood. The concrete divider was only a few inches above the sloshing water.

Somehow, Rob and his driver managed a tightrope walk across the lake the underpass had become, balancing on the concrete divider.

When they reached the other side, one of the newscasters, a guy in a red rain slicker, stuck a microphone in his face and asked him to tell him what happened. Was he afraid? Stunned, Rob shook his head and moved toward the cop cars. Behind him, he could hear the driver talking to the reporter.

At the first police car, a uniformed officer got out from behind the steering wheel. She shut the door behind her and held a hand above the bill of her cap to further shield her from the rain. She was young, maybe midtwenties, with short black hair and a stout and sturdy build.

"You okay, sir?"

Rob nodded. "Yeah, I guess." He smiled. "Didn't expect a swim this early in the morning."

The officer didn't laugh. "Where were you headed? We might be able to take you, or at the very least, we can summon a taxi for you."

And Rob opened his mouth to say, "To the airport" and then shut it again.

One thought stood out in his head. *I could have drowned.* He looked toward the Lincoln, which was filled now with water up to the middle of the windshield.

"Sir? You need us to get you somewhere?"

Rob debated, thinking of a young man, perhaps out in this same rain, getting almost as drenched as he was. He opened his mouth again to speak, unsure of how he could or should answer her question.

What he said now could very well determine the course of the rest of his life.

Chapter One

"This one time, my dad and I were fighting. This was when I was, oh, about sixteen, I guess, and we were going round and round about some damn thing—who remembers now?—but I very clearly recall getting exasperated with him and asking, 'What do you *want* from me?'

"And you know what he said? He smiled very sweetly, and for a moment I was taken in by it. See, Dad was pretty stingy with the smiles. So I smiled back, completely innocent. And then he says, without ever losing that sweet smile, 'What do I want from you? Your absence.'

"And then he turned and walked out of the room. Three weeks later, I was out of there." Jasper poured another cosmopolitan for Lacy from the pitcher on the glass coffee table.

"Whoa!" She cautioned him as he filled the tumbler higher and higher. "I want to be able to walk out of here tonight." Lacy flipped a curtain of black hair back from her face and took a sip. "Ah, you do have a kind of magic touch. I put the same ingredients together and, I swear, it'll come out nothing like this." She took another sip and closed her eyes in ecstasy. "Damn." After a short pause, she asked, "Now, tell me for real. Is that story even true? Was your father really that mean?"

It was Jasper's turn to close his eyes. What rose up behind his eyelids was an image of his father—dark wavy hair, pale blue-gray eyes, and perfect teeth—smiling so kindly, so lovingly. Jasper had hardly ever been the beneficiary of a smile like that growing up, and its effect was powerful, almost jarring, bringing for the tiniest of moments a certain joy. And then Dad said what he did.

How Jasper wished he could say it was all made-up, an attention-getting fiction, a melodramatic tale of family dysfunction.

A lump formed in Jasper's throat, and his eyes began to well. He told himself, *No, I'm not giving the man that power. I won't.* He took a big gulp of his cocktail and swallowed. When he opened his eyes, he drew in a big breath and smiled at his best friend and roommate, Lacy, and said, "I'm just being dramatic." He snorted with laughter that wasn't real and then told her, "My dad never got over what happened in our family. So it was always kind of hard for him, I think, to give me the love I wanted so bad. I think of him now as someone swimming in grief and never able to rise up from it, you know?"

Lacy smiled—and her smile was truly kind and loving, so Jasper had no fear that her next words would be anything other than supportive and sympathetic. "That poor man."

"Yeah, that poor man." Jasper turned his gaze to the big flat-screen in front of them. People always felt sorry for his dad when Jasper was growing up alone under his care. In fact, many of them said those very words, "That poor man, left to raise that little boy all alone." And it *was* sad, but was Jasper wrong to feel he had somehow gotten lost in the shuffle, nothing more than an excess coda in the story of his family's tragedy? "Sh," he hushed Lacy. "It's starting."

As one, they both set down their drinks to watch the series finale of Ryan Murphy's FX series, *The*

Assassination of Gianni Versace. Jasper and Lacy had been recording the series since it began a few weeks ago and would sit down every Tuesday, the only night they both had off at the same time, to watch the latest edition of Murphy's *American Crime Story* opus.

It was no secret that Jasper had a huge crush on series star and portrayer of murderer Andrew Cunanan, Darren Criss.

When Lacy found out about Jasper's pining for the former *Glee* star, she'd joked, "Isn't that kind of masturbatory?"

"What do you mean?" Jasper asked, batting his lashes innocently.

"Oh, don't pretend. You can beat off to a picture of Darren Criss, or you can look in a mirror. Same difference, just about."

They'd both laughed. Inside, Jasper was thrilled that Lacy thought he looked like the TV star. Even though Criss was Asian American and Jasper himself was Italian American, he conceded that maybe there was a passing resemblance.

The show began and, for the next forty-five minutes or so, the living room of their shared one-bedroom in the Rogers Park neighborhood of Chicago was quiet.

When the show ended and the pitcher of cosmos was empty, Lacy looked over at Jasper. "It's such a sad story, really."

"What? You feel sorry for Cunanan?"

"I feel sorry for everybody. But yeah, maybe a little bit. He was batshit crazy. He wanted the things we all want—love, security, a home. He just didn't know how to go about getting them."

Jasper shrugged. "I guess. Though I think Versace's sister, Donatella, would beg to differ."

"Yeah, she probably sees him as a murderous wannabe, a hanger-on, a ruiner of lives."

"Which he was. All of those things."

Lacy sighed and stood. She was a little shaky and had to grab the arm of the couch for support. "I should probably start getting ready."

It was their custom, after a little TV on Tuesdays, to head out to a couple of the gay bars a bit farther south in the Andersonville neighborhood. Lacy was Jasper's trusty wingwoman, and sometimes he felt sorry for her. She never complained about always being at Jasper's side, helping him vet and judge the young men on offer at the bars on a Tuesday night with nary a chance for her to meet someone, unless she wanted to go the lesbian route, which she'd tried once or twice without, according to her, much success or satisfaction. "I like dick as much as you do," she'd confided to Jasper.

"Is that even possible?" Jasper had responded, laughing.

*

When the TV was turned off, the magazines arranged on the coffee table, the dishes stacked in the sink, and the apartment looking okay in case a visitor should come back later, Jasper and Lacy stood in the small entryway of their vintage one-bedroom apartment, appraising each other's looks in the mirror on the front closet door.

Jasper wished Lacy would stop with the goth-chick crap. For one, she was past thirty by a couple of years. Take away the black dye job, the thick eyeliner, the violet lipstick, the black taffeta, leather, and lace of her ensemble, and you'd have a soccer mom, one with mousy brown hair, wide hips, and a flat chest. The description,

Jasper knew, wasn't kind, but it was on target. And it wasn't that he advocated she go for the soccer-mom look. Not at all. He knew she could cut her long hair, let it go back to its natural brown, amp it up with some golden highlights, and she'd look great. Throw on some skinny jeans, low boots, and a blousy top. With the right makeup and jewelry, she'd probably look a good decade younger.

The goth business was so over. It had been over since Jasper was a kid.

"You put so little effort into it," Lacy said, her gaze affixed to Jasper's green eyes in the mirror. She applied her purple lipstick and blotted it with a Kleenex.

"What do you mean?" Jasper knew, but he wanted to hear. He could always use a little extra confidence before setting out into the jungle of gay bars in Chicago, where there was always someone a little better waiting around a corner.

"Look at you. You take a shower, throw on a pair of Levi's and a white T-shirt, a pair of Cons, and you're good to go. You look like you just got off work from a *GQ* fashion shoot."

Jasper laughed. "Oh come on, sister. You're too kind."

"I am not and you know it."

Jasper looked at himself in the mirror—the wavy dark hair, the pale green eyes, the slight but strong build. He wondered how many more years past his current age of twenty-five he'd be able to enjoy such effortless handsomeness. He wasn't being vain—he knew nothing lasted forever. If he could pull a Dorian Gray, he would, right this very moment, freezing this look in place. "Ah." He waved Lacy's praise away. "You and I both know nothing lasts forever."

Lacy opened the front door, hoisting her bag up to her shoulder. "Which is why you should make the most of it." She giggled and raised her eyebrows.

"What do you mean?"

"Old Andrew Cunanan had the right idea, He just had poor, if you'll pardon the pun, execution."

"Oh, you're terrible, Muriel," Jasper said, echoing Toni Collette in a favorite movie of theirs, *Muriel's Wedding*.

"Seriously, though, you should see if you can't find yourself a nice sugar daddy. Someone who will get you out of this shithole—"

"—and into the palace I deserve?"

"Exactly. Why not? Do it right and you can have all your dreams come true and never have to lift a finger. You're good-looking enough, Jazz, and you know it."

He didn't know if he *did* know it, but the idea had occurred to him watching the Cunanan movie. If Andrew hadn't been such a fucked-up loon, maybe he'd be doing fine today, sipping a glass of expensive wine while watching the sun set from some fabulous mansion in the tropics or on the Riviera coast.

Jasper shook his head. He was a shopgirl, refolding clothes at the Nordstrom Rack store downtown. What would he even talk about with some rich dude? At least Cunanan had a line of bull, a persona to draw on. Jasper grew up poor in southern Illinois, with a welder father who ignored him and a tragic history trailing him.

He wasn't good enough for some rich guy. He *was* good enough, however, for a hot young guy. And that's precisely what he intended to find tonight.

"Let's go," he said to Lacy, taking her arm and leading her out the door.

*

Where was Lacy?

Jasper leaned against a barstool, one cheek on it, one cheek off, swaying softly to the music in Carlton's, the newest gay bar in Andersonville. The music was something vintage he knew Lacy would love, something she'd introduced him to, an eighties band called ABC. Right now, they were singing a tune called "The Look of Love." Through the haze of his vodka-addled brain, one of the lyrics came through to him and made him shiver a little—the one about true love being the one thing he couldn't find. He closed his eyes. *Don't be maudlin. Don't feel sorry for yourself. You're young yet. You'll get that look one day.*

Lacy was nowhere around. Jasper took another sip of his cosmo, and the supersweet drink caused a little frisson of nausea to pass through him. He needed to get home to his bed with its flannel sheet and old, worn quilt.

Hadn't Lacy said something about an hour ago about being tired herself? About grabbing a cab on Clark Street? Jasper nodded in agreement with himself. And as always, she'd wanted Jasper to come home with her, although she'd never, ever say it. For the two of them to go home, kick off their shoes, have a nightcap, and maybe watch a little *Golden Girls* on Hulu. Maybe it would be one of those nights when one or the other would sneak into the other's bed, and they'd hold each other until dawn crept in, two bugs in a rug, as Lacy would put it.

But Jasper had sent her away, his need for male companionship too great. There'd been a beefy redhead with a beard eyeing him. Going home with Lacy would have felt too much like failure. And yet, the redhead had disappeared.

And here *he* was, still drunk and empty-handed. The bar was due to close in a few minutes. The bartender had already brought up the lights and made the now-familiar call, "You don't have to go home, but you can't stay here."

Maybe this moment, right here and right now, was the true failure.

He swiveled in the stool, appraising himself in the mirror behind the bar. In the wan light, he looked older than his years, tired. The fresh look he'd had when they'd left the apartment was gone, swallowed up by too much booze and fatigue. He thought of himself as Neely O'Hara from another of the favorite classic movies he shared with Lacy, *Valley of the Dolls*.

The music stopped, and another song didn't follow. Jasper pulled his phone out and saw that it was only a couple of minutes before two. There were four messages from Lacy. He supposed they were all missives designed to make him feel guilty, despite her encouraging him to have a good time and not worry about her when she left a while back. "I won't wait up," she'd said with a wink as she took her departure. Yet he knew that she'd lie in bed, listening for the sound of his key in the lock.

The bartender, a guy who called himself Luc but whom Jasper knew for a fact was really named George, leaned over the bar. "We're closing up in a few, bro. If you want to come back to my place after we close, it's cool. I got some weed..."

Jasper eyed the guy, who was probably a good ten years older than Jasper. He mulled over the offer but with a distinct lack of enthusiasm. He'd taken guys like Luc up too many times. "Better than nothing," he was learning, was a lie. In spite of the tight wifebeater tank, the tiger tattoo around his pumped-up left bicep, and the thick shock of bedhead platinum blond, George looked worn out, the crow's-feet around his bloodshot eyes prominent, the sagging of his cheeks bearing testimony to his excesses. A phrase Lacy used came to mind: "Mutton dressed as lamb."

The saddest thing? Jasper *had* gone home with him before. He knew the weed was just the start. That would be followed by a shot of G, maybe a pipeful of meth, both of which Jasper would politely refuse with an "I'm good." Even at his young age, he'd seen too many lives destroyed by those drugs.

Jasper didn't need that stuff, especially not if it made you look like old George here. And it would, Jasper knew, because he'd seen that story played out far too many times. Sad.

"Ah, I think I'm gonna just head home and crash."

Luc/George frowned, rubbing at a sticky spot on the bar with a rag. "If you change your mind, the offer's always good. And you know where I live. It's walking distance, over on Argyle." He winked, grinned, and walked away to do whatever he needed to do to finalize another night at the bar.

Jasper wondered how many other guys he'd invited over. Another thing he knew about George/Luc—he was a proponent of the old saw "the more the merrier." He also wasn't picky.

With the lights on, Carlton's was revealed for the sad little room it really was. Jasper said, "I'm beat. Gonna head up north—home." He hoisted himself the rest of the way off the barstool and headed out into the night.

Clark Street, at this hour, was deserted. Even the traffic had slowed to a car or two every few minutes. Jasper had a couple of choices. He could hoof it over to the L stop at Foster, a few blocks south and east, or he could wait for a bus to come along. A number 22 could roll up within five minutes—or an hour. This late, the buses were unpredictable. Two could show up, one behind the other, and then there wouldn't be another for over an hour.

What the hell? He had his phone and could peruse Instagram or Twitter while he waited for the bus. He had a Gregg Olsen true-crime book on his Kindle app. He was too tired to walk the half dozen or more blocks to the L. Besides, who knew how long he might have to wait for a train once he got to the station anyway? It would all balance out, right?

Even though it was late March and Chicago could be brutal at this time of year, the evening was actually sort of pleasant. Jasper had worn his biker jacket and had sensibly brought along a stocking cap and gloves, which he now donned. The air was crisp, yet a little damp from the piles of dirty melting snow in the gutter. The moon above was a wisp of a crescent, silver. Jasper knew there were stars up there, but light pollution hid them from his view. Louise, the next-door neighbor who had pretty much raised him, had once told him, "The stars are always there, honey. You might not be able to see 'em, but they're there, just waiting for you to bask in their brilliance. You remember that." Jasper smiled.

He was about to post a selfie he'd just taken, his cheeks high with winter color, when a black car guided to the curb. It was a Lexus, and the windows were tinted.

Jasper took a cautious step back as the window on the passenger side descended.

"You need a lift?" a gruff voice floated out from the car's interior, one that sounded scarred by too many cigarettes.

Jasper stooped down a little to peer inside. It was too dark to see much, but the dashboard light illuminated enough to reveal a pot-bellied guy behind the driver's wheel. He had a head of thick, short salt-and-pepper hair and a goatee, almost all white. He was smiling, but as Jasper moved a little closer to the car, he could see the smile didn't reach the guy's dark eyes.

Jasper shivered. "I'm okay. The bus should be along any minute." Jasper peered south on Clark, which was woefully empty.

Way down, he spied a taxi pulling over to pick up a fare. He wished he had enough money to afford a cab.

"The bus? C'mon, man! You'll freeze your ass off. Where you goin'?"

The guy had his car radio tuned to some easy-listening station. Elevator music floated out. Jasper glanced behind himself, wishing someone else would emerge from the bar.

"Just up north a bit. Rogers Park."

"It's on my way. Hop in." The guy leaned across the seat to open the door.

And now Jasper was confronted with a dilemma he knew well. The doing-something-I-shouldn't-but-doing-it-anyway-just-to-be-polite thing. Jasper had gone home with guys he wasn't attracted to in the past because it would have been more awkward to say no. He invariably regretted the choice he'd made and always told himself it made no sense, because he only gave the poor guy hope when there was none to be had.

These were the thoughts that accompanied him as he slid into the Lexus and closed the door.

Immediately, Jasper felt too warm. And the guy's resemblance to another killer, one known well around

Chicago and not *nearly* as sexy as Andrew Cunanan, rose up to chill Jasper despite the car's heat—John Wayne Gacy.

Gacy was dead. But from his reading, Jasper thought this was just the kind of move Gacy would have pulled, back when he lived over on the west side. And Jasper would have been just his type too.

"Too warm?"

Jasper nodded. His mouth was suddenly dry.

"I'm Jerry, by the way. Jerry Mathias." He stuck his hand out, and Jasper shook it.

"Jazz." Jasper wasn't going to give him a last name, nor even his real first one.

"Jazz man!" Jerry sang and then laughed. "You know the song?"

Jasper shook his head, wondering if he could just hop out at the next stoplight or stop sign.

"Carole King!" He laughed. "She was probably before your time."

Jerry turned down the heat and clicked the radio off. "Where am I taking you, buddy?"

Jasper was about to blurt, "Uh-uh, you're not taking me anywhere." But then he realized the guy wanted to know where to drop him off; at least that's what he hoped. "You can just let me out at the corner of Ashland and Fargo. Is that okay?" He didn't want the guy to know exactly where he lived. He wasn't sure why. Lacy would say, "Just because you're paranoid doesn't mean they're not out to get you."

On the short ride north, though, Jasper had to let go of his paranoia and fear. The guy actually started to come across as sort of nice, warm in a fatherly way Jasper had never known. He asked Jasper all about his life, his work, his living situation, but nothing so personal that it was creepy.

And when they were nearing the intersection where Jasper would depart, the guy smiled at him and said, "Kid, you know I can drop you off at your front door. I'm *not* out to get you. I have a son older than you. Pretty as you are, you're way too young for the likes of me." He chuckled. "For one, I probably couldn't keep up with you even if you were interested, and number two, and don't take offense, but I like my men on the more mature side." He chuckled again. "Ones I don't have to explain who Carole King is."

"Make a left," Jasper said.

He directed Jerry to his front door. He was no longer worried about him. Jasper's gut told him the guy was harmless, and his gut was almost always right.

"Thanks." Jasper threw open the door.

"You're welcome. But kid?"

"Yeah?"

"You got lucky tonight. Old Jerry is as harmless as a pussycat. But the next car that pulls over might have a mountain lion in it, or worse."

"Good advice." Jasper swung his legs out of the vehicle.

"You take care now. Stay out of the bars. They'll make you old before your time."

Jasper looked over. "Is being old really so bad?" He felt heat rise to his face. "Not that I'm calling *you* old, of course—"

Jerry cut him off with a guffaw. "Ah, I'm old all right. Just turned sixty at Christmastime. No shame in that. But you want to enjoy your youth. I'm just saying, find another pretty boy your own age, and have the fireworks that you can only have in your twenties."

"I don't know what that means."

"I know. And you won't until you're my age. Good night, Jazz."

There was nothing more to say, so Jasper got out of the car. He stood for a long time, watching the black Lexus until it rounded the corner at Paulina.

Jasper turned toward his front door while groping around in his pocket for his keys. As he opened the door, he wondered what it would be like to drive a Lexus, to be warm on a winter's night, to offer sage advice to a pretty boy who had no idea about where his life was going. What kind of home would Jerry Mathias return to tonight? One of those mansions along the lakeshore in Evanston, Wilmette, Winnetka? Or would he turn south and head over to Lake Shore Drive and lay his head down in some tower in the sky, with city *and* lake views?

As he started up the stairs to his apartment, he heard the click of the dead bolt being thrown and the creak of his front door opening. Even though he couldn't see her, he could visualize Lacy in her quilted bathrobe, standing at the door, arms crossed. All the makeup tissued off her face, she'd look wan, a little frightened, her dark eyes bright. He'd seen this vision of her enough times to know what it looked like without actually seeing it.

She called down to him as he wearily mounted the stairs. "I'm so glad you're home. I was worried."

Jasper smirked and rolled his eyes. "I thought you weren't going to wait up."

"I didn't. I fell asleep and had a bad dream about you."

"Oh?" Jasper brushed by her in the doorway, heading for the living room. He plopped down on the couch to take his shoes off.

Lacy came to sit near him. "Yeah, I dreamed some guy picked you up in a black car. He drove you to some park along the lakefront."

Her words gave Jasper a chill, but he didn't want it to show. "Wouldn't be the first time." The lakeside parks along the north side of town were notorious for cruising and had been for many years.

"He slit your throat."

"Gah! That's horrible!"

"I know, right? I woke up crying."

Jasper moved down the couch and took Lacy in his arms, which is what he supposed she'd expected all along. He pulled away only long enough to say, "Want me to sleep with you tonight?"

She grinned. "You mean, like, as in sex?"

He punched her arm. "No, silly. And you know that's not what I meant."

She stood and held out her hand. "Come on, it's time for platonic bedtime. My favorite."

Jasper took her hand and followed her into her bedroom, pretending not to notice the look of sadness stamped on her doughy features.

Chapter Two

When Jasper awoke on Wednesday morning, he was in his own bed. The quality of the sunlight streaming in through the slats in his partially open mini blinds told him it was late morning. He sat up and yawned, stretching. Wednesdays he didn't need to be in at the store until after lunch. He remembered crawling into bed with Lacy last night. She'd wrapped her arms around him, spooning against his back, and he'd immediately fallen asleep.

What he didn't recall was getting up at some point and getting in his own bed. He supposed it must have happened during a late-night run to the bathroom.

Lately, Lacy was finding more and more excuses to get him into bed with her. Even if it was just platonic, Jasper knew it probably wasn't such a healthy thing and that he should put a stop to it, or at least curtail it. She already called him her "Will" and her "gay husband." She didn't need the additional encouragement of having him in her bed every night. How would she ever find a man of her own?

More importantly: How would he?

Besides, he'd made the dining room into his own bedroom—and it was only a few feet from Lacy's room. To get to the other, they need only traverse a distance of about thirty or so steps. They were close enough that they could talk to each other from their respective beds, as long as an L train wasn't thundering by.

As his feet hit the hardwood floor beneath his bed, he had three thoughts.

The first was coffee. He needed some desperately. When he'd moved in with Lacy, he hadn't even liked the stuff, but she quickly made an addict out of him. Now he just couldn't seem to get himself going without at least one good cup of dark roast in him, especially after a night of imbibing. Lacy turned up her nose at what he poured into his morning brew and called him a kid, but he still needed to "enhance" his morning joe with french vanilla creamer and not one, not two, but three teaspoons of sugar. "You're not drinking coffee. You're drinking a mocha shake," Lacy would chide him, the steam rising from her own unadulterated black coffee.

The second thought was *Who's watching me now?* Their apartment was on the second floor, same level as the L tracks. The three windows in Jasper's "bedroom" faced those tracks, and often because their building was very near the terminus of the Red Line at Howard, trains would wait for clearance into the busy final North Side station—right outside Jasper's windows. As easily as he could look out at the passengers, they could just as easily observe him.

He didn't worry much about exposure, standing up in only his Diesel trunks. He'd learned quickly that almost all the people on the trains weren't particularly interested in peering out the window—or into his. No, nearly every one of them had their faces downward, looking at either a phone, an e-reader, or a tablet. The world outside, Jasper sometimes thought, had gone out of fashion. It wasn't real unless it was posted on Facebook or Twitter.

So he didn't bother closing his blinds tight, even though the train, like some huffing monster, stood motionless right outside, almost close enough to touch. If people wanted to look at his skinny body, let them.

Meantime, coffee. He headed toward the kitchen with his third thought, which he voiced aloud. "It's awfully quiet in here."

Usually, Lacy was up before him and bustling around. She'd have music playing—maybe streaming some Chopin from a Spotify playlist. She would turn on lights and, if she didn't opt for music, turn on the TV, tuning it to the local news if she could stand it, a rerun of *I Love Lucy* if she wanted to escape. He seldom had to make coffee himself. He was even a little daunted by their French press, even though Lacy told him over and over it was the easiest way to make coffee. "It's idiotproof," she told him, "So I'm pretty sure you can handle it."

But Lacy must have had more to drink than he realized last night and was still sleeping it off. Save for the usual urban noises, the apartment was eerily still. Jasper felt quite alone, and it was unsettling. There were times when he pined for his own place, imagining a morning like this one when he could spread out and enjoy his solitude, but the truth was he liked having Lacy around, the noise she made, hell, the coffee she made.

After emptying his bladder, he headed back out to the kitchen to unravel the mystery of the French press. It wasn't so much using the thing that confounded him. He never knew how much coffee to grind to put in it. He was never sure if he should grind the beans finely or coarsely. Lacy always said, "Err on the side of strong." He set the teakettle filled with tap water on the stove to boil, ground enough coffee to fill the bottom quarter of the press, which looked like the amount Lacy would have put in, and went to check on her.

Her door was tightly shut, which made Jasper pause. This was unusual. Whether they shared a bed or not, she usually left her door partially open so if he wanted to wander in and talk to her, he could. Jasper's brow furrowed, and he tiptoed over to her door, listening.

He didn't expect to hear much. The doors in these old vintage buildings were heavy, solid affairs. They didn't allow much noise in or out. Jasper had been grateful for that in the past. He'd brought home more than a few noisy one-night stands, and it seemed Lacy had always slept through their encounters—and their moans and groans.

Or at least she never let on that she heard.

Jasper tried the knob. If she was really out, she wouldn't hear the door creak open. And if she was stirring, he could offer to bring her a cup of coffee in bed. He could be a really good roomie and see if she wanted toast with that horrible bitter orange marmalade she liked.

He wished Lacy had made the coffee. It always tasted better, kind of like how his cocktails were better when he was doing the mixing.

He and Lacy complemented each other, at least in the beverage department.

He swung the door open.

The room was dark, really dark. The blind, one of those old-fashioned kinds, had been pulled all the way to the sill. Only the thinnest glow of sunlight showed around its edges.

Jasper froze. His gut was processing things much more quickly than his mind, which was usually how it worked out.

The quiet was what really got to him. There were no sounds of breathing, or snoring, or tossing in bed.

It was just—still.

Jasper took a few steps toward the bed.

And then stopped again.

Something's wrong. He just knew it.

"Lace? Lacy? Don't mean to wake you, but..." But what? Jasper didn't know.

He took a few steps closer to the edge of Lacy's brass four-poster. Only a bit of her black hair stuck out above the covers. The sight chilled Jasper, who suddenly wanted nothing more than to turn and run from the room.

"Lacy?" His whisper was urgent, willing her to stir, to throw back the covers and laugh.

He reached behind him, groping for the overhead light switch. He found it and switched on the light.

The overturned prescription bottle on the bedside table was what he noticed first. He drew in a deep breath and closed his eyes, keeping still for a moment. He knew the end of this story. He just didn't want to accept it.

It was hard to swallow over the lump in his throat, his suddenly dry mouth. He started to say Lacy's name once more, but couldn't seem to find the spit or the voice to do it.

With a trembling hand, he picked up the pill bottle. Ambien. Lacy had struggled with insomnia ever since he knew her. The Ambien usually did the trick for her, although she'd sometimes sleepwalk at night and make herself a bowl of pasta or some scrambled eggs. They'd laugh about it, but Jasper was always afraid she'd burn the damn place down.

He didn't want to look at her.

So he peered down at the bottle in his hand. Took the cap off and turned it upside down. Nothing fell out.

Jasper had no idea when she'd last refilled the medication at CVS, so he had no clue how many pills were in the bottle. *Just look at the date on the bottle, dummy,* he told himself. That would give him some idea of how many pills should be in there.

But he didn't want to know. Because, maybe she refilled them yesterday, or the day before, and there would've been at least thirty of the tablets.

"Lacy!" It was no longer a question but a cry, helpless, wavering.

He dropped the amber pill bottle to the floor and reached for the bedclothes. With a great intake of breath, like ripping the bandage off a wound, he yanked back the covers.

He wasn't sure what to expect. What he wanted to see was Lacy staring up at him, her eyes twinkling. She'd point and laugh at him, crying out, "Gotcha!"

What he feared seeing was an ashen Lacy, eyes bulging and staring unseeing up at the ceiling, a line of vomit dribbling out of the corner of her mouth.

But what he saw was Lacy looking as though she were deeply asleep. For once, her brow was untroubled. For once, her face looked young, innocent, and serene. For once, she seemed at peace.

Her color was good—she was always pale, but her skin seemed to glow. Maybe that was simply Jasper's imagination. Her eyes were closed, and her hair fanned out on the pillow behind her, a sharp black contrast to the pristine white of the pillowcase.

He looked down at her chest, and for a moment he thought he saw the rise and fall of it beneath her white eyelet nightgown.

And then he gasped and stumbled a step backward as it sunk in—her chest was *not* moving.

He took a moment, then reached out and touched her, laid a hand on her cheek.

He snatched his hand back as though burned. But her skin was icy, waxy, and curiously hard beneath his fingertips.

"Oh God," he whispered. He thought not only of the sleeping pills, but all they'd drunk the night before. A cold, clinical voice whispered in his ear, "The combination of the sleeping pills and alcohol could be lethal."

"Could be?" he wondered aloud.

He then grabbed her wrist, hoping against hope he'd feel a faint pulse. But there was nothing.

When he pressed his ear to her chest, the tears now leaking from his eyes, the silence of the morning mocked him.

"No," he said and stuffed a fist to his mouth.

He hit her then, one out-of-control, frenzied punch to the chest. "Dammit, Lace! How could you?"

He screamed as the teakettle began to whistle in the kitchen.

He hurried out of the room to quiet it.

And then he went to his bedside table, picked up his phone, and called 911.

Chapter Three

The funeral home was old school. In a converted turn-of-the-century (twentieth century, that is) white brick and white-trimmed mansion only steps away from Lake Michigan and squarely on the border of Rogers Park and Edgewater, the home had a large front porch, massive picture windows, a gate with stone pillars, and an expansive east-facing front yard, bordered by carefully sculpted shrubbery.

As Jasper hurried up the front walk for Lacy's wake, he paused for a moment, almost overcome by how unreal all of this felt. Sure, he could hear the traffic behind him on Sheridan Road, and just beyond that ebb and flow, a more natural ebb and flow of waves crashing into boulders. Children screamed from a playground at a nearby elementary school. Their recess seemed somehow wrong and added to the surreal aspect of the morning.

After he'd phoned 911 that awful morning a few days ago, he'd called Lacy's parents. Even though he'd lived with their daughter for a few years and thought he knew her like a sister, he'd never met the people who'd brought her up. He knew only that they lived somewhere on the West Coast, Southern California, a town in the Coachella Valley called Indian Wells. Lacy's father had been an attorney before he retired, and her mother had always stayed home to take care of her, despite having a teaching degree. Like Jasper, Lacy was an only child.

And Jasper sucked in a breath as a memory assailed him. *You're not an only child. Well, you are now, but once upon a time, there was a sister, and another sibling on the way.* A grainy front-page photograph Jasper had stared at many times of a ransacked used-furniture store popped into his head, the image like something out of a nightmare. Before he could push it away, he saw again the dark splashes and splatters on the floor and an old couch that he knew were his mother's and his sister's blood. There was an old, worn newspaper article, too, that he'd once found hidden in his father's sock drawer. It was so creased where it had been folded it was all but ready to come apart in his hands. The newsprint felt soft, almost like fabric. Jasper, because he never really remembered the killings, had read over the article so many times as a kid that he had it memorized.

The details were horrific. How could they not be?

He stood for a moment more on the expansive front porch to collect himself, facing the large, heavy oak double doors with their spiral design and black wrought-iron handles. Leaded glass windows at eye level provided a distorted, blurry view inside.

The sky behind him was gunmetal gray. The air smelled of imminent snow. The temperature that morning hovered around twenty degrees. A wind—sharp, arctic—blew across the lake, propelling him to open the door.

He went inside.

The interior of the funeral home was hushed. Very softly, classical music—Brahms, maybe—played over speakers built into the ceiling. In the air was an almost sickening aroma of cut flowers, floral "tributes" he supposed they'd be called here. He'd thought briefly of sending a Venus flytrap. Lacy would have appreciated it.

In front of him was a long corridor, carpeted in plush mauve, that led to the back of the house. At its end were large floor-to-ceiling windows that looked out upon a back garden, brown and dead-looking in March. The walls were papered in cream with a subtle stripe.

To his left and right were identical doors, similar to the oak front door but unadorned by any design. In front of one was a sign reading "Esther Purdy."

In front of the other was a sign reading "Heather Burroughs."

Where was Lacy? *Am I in the wrong place?*

And then it came back to him: her real name was Heather, which she despised and had threatened him with castration if he ever used it in her presence.

If ever a name could've been more wrong for a person, it was Heather for Lacy. She was *not* a Heather. Heathers were blonde, the cheerleader or the majorette. Heathers were not goth. Heathers got married to doctors or lawyers and had 2.5 tow-headed children and lived in suburbs like Wilmette or Kenilworth.

Heathers didn't commit suicide.

The coroner never said she actually ended her own life. No, the death certificate read Accidental Overdose.

But Jasper knew the truth, even though Lacy's parents didn't want to accept it. They clung to the fact that she didn't leave a note, that her passing was sudden and unexpected.

But Jasper had checked that pill bottle. It had been refilled the morning before Lacy's death. She'd taken them all, on top of a belly swimming with vodka.

Jasper would always wonder when she had done it. Had it been when he lay in bed next to her? He shuddered.

He opened the door where "Heather Burroughs" lay.

Seeing the open casket, an elegant pewter lined with ivory satin, shocked him so much that he took a wavering step back and caught his breath. For a moment, he simply thought of turning and running straight back outside. Once there, he'd dash for the L stop at Argyle, board a northbound train, and head for home, where he could nurse his grief in his own bed with reruns of *The Golden Girls* playing.

The thought was comforting and tempting, save for the fact that he seriously wondered if he could continue to live in the small vintage one-bedroom he'd shared with her. They'd been thrilled when they found it, even if it had meant converting the dining room into a bedroom for Jasper. He thought he could use the actual bedroom now. But no, he couldn't. It was where she'd drawn her last breath. The possibility that she drew that breath with him lying beside her was almost too horrible to contemplate.

What was worse, though, was thinking she might have died in bed alone.

He took a deep breath, closing his eyes for a moment, and counted in his head until five as he slowly exhaled.

It helped. A little.

You have to look at her. It's the decent thing to do. All eyes are on you at the moment, anyway. They're not expecting her roommate and best friend to run from the room like a coward. Move! Step up to the casket and say goodbye.

Even though he didn't want to, desperately, he forced his feet to move toward her.

He paused in front of the casket, not looking down, and then he forced himself.

A bark of laughter escaped him, and he hushed it quickly with his palm. Behind him, conversation stopped for a moment, then started up again.

It's not her. The thought was a relief, a blessing.

Of course it was. His head told him so. But the young woman lying before him was not the Lacy he'd known—and loved.

Maybe this was Heather, at last the girl her parents had wanted.

The black hair was gone. In its place was a light brown with golden highlights. It curled around her cherubic face. Lacy had favored purple lipstick, heavy mascara and eyeliner, a deep "smoky" eye. Heather now wore pale blush on her cheeks and coral lip gloss. Her lids were painted with a subtle shade of brownish-green that complemented what Jasper assumed was her true, natural hair color.

She wore a white dress, almost bridal, trimmed in lace. A pale pink blanket was pulled up to just beneath her bosom.

She looks beautiful. But it's not her. Jasper couldn't tell if it was the sight of Lacy, so changed in death, or the overpowering smell of all the flowers around her making his stomach churn.

In her hands, she held a leather-bound edition of the Bible. A silver cross pendant was woven between her fingers.

Jasper couldn't help himself. He began to laugh. It started as a little chuckle at first, then bloomed into a guffaw, then a hysterical, unstoppable force. Tears streamed down his face, his eyes wide. He stuffed a fist to his mouth, yet still was helpless to stop what wouldn't be denied.

She was an atheist!

After a moment, he was able to slow the laughter. He wiped his eyes and turned to look at the people in the room behind him. There were slack jaws and frowns. Those that weren't confused by his display were appalled. Again, no one was speaking.

Jasper rushed from the room.

Down the hall, he found a bathroom and ducked inside. He bent over the sink and splashed his face with icy water again and again. After he dried himself with coarse paper towels from an automatic dispenser in the wall, he regarded himself in the mirror.

His color was high. If he didn't know better, he looked as though he was enjoying himself.

He shook his head. *You need to go home. No matter how it looks, you cannot do this. You will write a very nice, apologetic letter to her parents. You will send flowers, irises, Lacy's favorite, today.*

But you just can't stay here.

When he stepped out of the bathroom, someone was waiting for him. An older man.

Jasper tried to thread his way around the guy. "Did you want to go in?" Jasper gestured toward the open bathroom.

"No. I was waiting for you." The guy eyed him. He was probably a good twenty years older than Jasper, but as inappropriate as it was at a time like this, Jasper couldn't help noticing how sexy he was. Trim, a little on the short side, it was obvious, even in his impeccably tailored black suit, he was in very good, and very powerful, shape. Jasper was certain those weren't shoulder pads testing the seams at the tops of his arms.

He had kind eyes. And they were the most amazing shade of pale gray. Jasper had seen a husky once with eyes like that; he couldn't say he'd ever seen anything like it on a human being. Those eyes were mesmerizing, arresting, and chilling, framed in long, black lashes.

His hair was silver, shorn close on the sides with a bit more on top, spiked with some gel.

He wore a fashionable five-o'clock shadow that Jasper couldn't deny he wanted to feel—either with his fingers or against his own smooth cheeks.

"For me?" Jasper smiled. "I'm sorry. Do I know you?"

He simply smiled enigmatically. "Probably not. But I bet I know you. You're Jasper, Heather's roommate, right?"

"Yeah. And you are?"

"I'm Robert. Robert Burroughs." He extended his hand.

Jasper gripped the warm hand, slightly soft and a little damp. He didn't take his eyes off Robert the whole time, and the "whole time" was much longer than the duration of a handshake for most guys. It sent a shiver through Jasper.

"Burroughs?" Jasper had a terrifying thought. *What if this is her dad? Good Lord, I'm flirting with Lacy's dad! At her funeral!* The very thought caused beads of sweat to pop out on Jasper's forehead. He held in a giddy burst of laughter. "Are you, um, related to Lacy? Er, Heather?"

Please don't say you're her father.

"I'm her uncle Rob. Did she never mention me?"

Jasper wracked his brain. One thing neither of them did much of was talk about their respective families. They liked to believe they were each other's family now, "chosen family" was the term they used. The idea, the memory of this, brought a lump to Jasper's throat, bringing home for real that his best friend was gone. "I'm not sure."

"It's okay if she didn't. I hadn't seen her in quite some time. My schedule doesn't afford me much opportunity to see family, as much as I might want to." He smiled, and Jasper noticed the sadness around his eyes despite it. Robert went on softly, "I wish I'd had one more chance to talk to her, to tell her how much I loved her. I'm afraid she didn't know."

Jasper nodded. "Me too. If I could just talk to her one more time, maybe we wouldn't be here."

Robert cocked his head. "No?"

Jasper didn't want to disabuse him of the notion that Lacy had *not* killed herself, if that was what he was choosing to believe. So he simply said, "Who knows?"

"Heather used to write sometimes, a long time ago. She'd shoot me a text, you know, a birthday emoji or a holiday one. We were close when she was a kid. I used to take her places with me whenever I could. Her parents never really got her, you know?"

"Oh, I know."

"They were always trying to change her. Like, she was left-handed naturally, and they worked and worked and worked on getting her to use her right. They tried to get her to hang out with what they deemed the popular girls. They bought her American Girl dolls when all she wanted was a set of paints and a good book, preferably horror. I could stand here all day and tell you how little my brother and sister-in-law knew their girl. But I won't.

"I just wish I'd stayed in better touch with her. Once my career took off, back when she was just becoming a teenybopper, I kind of got preoccupied and we lost touch." He paused and Jasper noticed the tears standing in his incredible eyes. Unexpectedly, he laughed. "When she was a little girl, and I mean like three or four, she would sigh and say, 'Woe is me.' What little girl says that?"

"Lacy. It so figures."

"You call her Lacy. Why?"

"That's how she referred to herself. She was even thinking of legally changing her name. She hated Heather."

Robert nodded. "I get that. I never thought of her as a Heather. I'm glad she found something else." He glanced over his shoulder into the viewing room. "I wish they'd respected that."

I do too. Jasper felt, suddenly, even sadder. For his own loss, sure, but more for Lacy's loss. The rest of her life. She could have done so much. She could have been happy. He just knew it.

He placed his hand on Robert's shoulder. "Look, I intended to stay longer, but I need to get out of here. This place is too oppressive. And it honestly feels like someone else is being waked, not the girl I know. So I'm gonna book. But it was nice to talk to you."

Robert nodded. "Will you be at the funeral tomorrow morning?"

The funeral was set for one of Rogers Park's Catholic churches. Then they'd fly the body back to California for burial in the family plot.

It was all wrong. All not what Lacy would have chosen.

Jasper shook his head. "No. I don't think so. This isn't her. I think I'll just remember her as I knew her."

Jasper turned away, feeling on the verge of tears. He didn't want to cry in front of Lacy's uncle—or anyone else gathered at the funeral home, for that matter.

As he reached the door, Robert's voice stopped him. "Jasper?"

He turned.

"Would you mind if I came with you? I need to get out of here too."

Jasper smiled through his tears. "No, I wouldn't mind. I'd like the company."

Robert hurried to join him. "Maybe we can go get a drink. Toast to Heather's—" He stopped himself. "Lacy's memory."

"That sounds nice. Come on. I know just the place."

And Robert followed him out into the cold.

The snow had begun to fall.

Chapter Four

Jasper had no idea what to do with this well-dressed, affluent-seeming man who was old enough to be his father. Robert Burroughs was a marginal step up from being a stranger. The only thing that kept him in Jasper's esteem was that he was a link to Lacy.

Jasper had been walking rapidly toward the L stop at Granville, head bowed against the biting wind, when Robert caught up. He held up his phone so Jasper could make out an app with a map and a little car on it. "I've phoned an Uber," he said. "It's too cold for public transportation." He smiled, and his gaze drifted upward to the L station a couple blocks west of them. "I'm guessing that's what you had in mind."

Of course it was what he had in mind, but Jasper took the tiniest bit of offense. He could have been headed for his car, couldn't he? Perhaps parked right around the corner? Did he look *that* poor? That he couldn't afford the humblest of junkers? His brain, forever reeling him back to earth, told him, *Dude, you are that poor.* He was on the verge of expressing his indignation verbally, but the realization made him hold his tongue. Robert was simply doing him a kindness. So what if he assumed Jasper was heading for the train, which he could hear the rattle of at this very moment? The assumption was correct.

Again, so what if he appeared poor? The truth was he *couldn't* afford a car, not even a piece-of-shit one with

100,000 miles on it. Gas, taxes, registration, insurance, parking fees, and city stickers alone would eat up too much of his pay to even consider the idea of private transportation. Besides, it *was* freezing. The temperature had dropped what seemed like at least ten degrees since he'd gone into the funeral home. The snow was coming down hard now and accumulating fast on the frozen concrete. He shivered.

"Thanks. I'd love a lift." He eyed Robert. *What is it with me and older guys giving me a ride suddenly?* In Jasper's mind's eye, he pictured Jerry Mathias, who had given him a ride home on the last night of his best friend's life.

"We should go wait in front of the funeral home." Robert did an about-face and started back from where they'd come.

Jasper turned too and followed. At least they could wait on the porch, where they'd have a bit of shelter from the wind off the lake and the big, fluffy flakes floating down from the dark gray sky. They were the kind of snowflakes that melted on contact, drenching you as quickly as a summer storm. Already, water trickled down Jasper's face from his hair.

He'd be glad to get to some shelter, but there wasn't time to even make it up the front steps of the funeral home.

A black Lincoln Continental glided to the curb about a block north of the place and discreetly flashed its lights.

"Our chariot awaits." Robert gestured toward the car.

Jasper knew the difference between Uber and UberX. The latter were much finer cars, more like limousines. The difference in cost was considerable too.

Robert opened the door for him, and Jasper hopped inside, grateful for the warmth.

Then Robert slid in next to him, so close their shoulders touched. Jasper got a little tingle from the closeness. And he loved the smell of the man. He recognized the scent, even if he couldn't afford it—Equipage by Hermes. They carried it at Nordstrom and sometimes got a few bottles in at the Rack, but it was still too expensive for him, even with his discount. He was more of an Axe man, much to his chagrin.

"Where to?" Robert shut the door with a *thunk*, silencing all the noise around them. It was suddenly so still, and the quiet made Jasper feel out of place, as though he'd stepped into another realm. Indeed, maybe he had.

And, although he'd said earlier he had someplace in mind, Jasper's actual mind was a blank. He thought for a minute, and an idea came to him, as though it had been there all along. He *did* know just the place after all. He only hoped it was open—and that Robert wouldn't be uncomfortable in a gay bar. Jasper leaned forward a bit. "Do you know where Wishful Drinking is?"

The driver, a well-coifed hipster type in a black suit, no tie, and sporting a man-bun, eyed Jasper in the rearview mirror. "No."

Jasper eyed him back, wondering if he was being truthful. It didn't matter. "Just head north on Sheridan a couple miles or so. Turn left on Jarvis."

The driver checked the traffic, now sparse because of the snow and the weekday afternoon, and smoothly and wordlessly executed a U-turn.

They headed north.

Robert surprised him, laying his hand on top of Jasper's. *Good Lord, is he putting the moves on me?* Jasper pretended to cough so he could move his own hand discreetly away. It wasn't that he minded Robert's touch, but it seemed somehow wrong in light of where they'd just come from.

"So where are you taking me? I love the name, by the way. I assume I can get a scotch there?"

Jasper nodded, although he'd never had scotch in his life. "It's a little neighborhood place around the corner from where Lacy and I live. Lived." Jasper looked out the window to hide the tears that sprang to his eyes.

"Where everybody knows your name?"

"Something like that." Jasper got the reference to the old sitcom *Cheers*, but it was also true. He and Lacy had started many a pub crawl at Wishful Drinking and had wound up many a night there, too, on the opposite end of an outing. It was a simple long room with scuffed hardwood floors, an ancient and massive mahogany bar with a brass footrail, a few stools, and a cluster of about a half dozen small table-and-chair sets. At one end of the bar was a statue of David. People decorated him for holidays with feather boas, rainbow flags, tinsel, Easter bonnets, and the like.

The snow was really coming down, almost whiteout conditions. Jasper was glad they didn't have to travel far and that it was nearly a straight shot. His concern over bringing Robert to a gay bar had vanished the moment the older man had laid his hand atop Jasper's.

He wondered why Lacy had never told him about her gay uncle, or "guncle," as the parlance these days sometimes dictated. It seemed like something that should have come up in conversation. "I have an uncle who's a big old 'mo, just like you!" she might have said early on in their acquaintance. And maybe she had and Jasper had just forgotten.

They pulled up in front of the bar.

"This is it?" Robert sounded disappointed, peering out at the little bar halfway up Jarvis Avenue and located on the ground floor of an old white-brick apartment building. There was a simple metal door and a black window, above which hung a pink neon sign reading Wishful Drinking. The neon stood out in an almost eerie way against the snow.

"This is it. Hope you weren't expecting more. I thought it would be quiet. Lacy and I used to come here a lot. Maybe it's more fitting that I remember her here instead of at that funeral parlor, where they'd made her into someone she wasn't."

Robert eyed him. "They did?" He seemed surprised.

Jasper turned a little to him. "You really didn't know her, did you?"

Robert shook his head a little, the movement almost imperceptible. He said quietly, "No. And now I really regret it." He stared out the window for a moment or two longer, and Jasper knew he was no longer looking at the bar. "We should get out." He leaned forward, his hand on the top of the front seat. "Thank you," he said to the driver.

"Watch your step getting out of the car," the driver said. "Stay warm."

"We'll try our best," Robert said.

Jasper followed him out of the car.

Once on the sidewalk, Robert crossed his arms over his chest as the wind whipped up, almost a scream off the lake a few blocks to the east. "Jesus!"

"I know, right? Let's get inside." Jasper didn't wait but headed for the heavy gray metal door. He pushed it open, certain Robert was right behind him.

The first thing he saw in the dimly lit bar was Lacy herself, seated at a small round table near the back. She was under a framed poster they used to laugh about that proclaimed It's Our Pleasure to Disgust You. She wore black, of course, but Jasper noticed she'd donned lace gloves, too, something she rarely pulled out of her closet. She peered at herself in a compact she held open in her hand. Her eyes, for just a moment, drifted up and met Jasper's. He took a step back. Jasper recalled he'd been with her when she'd found the gloves at a thrift store in the Ravenswood neighborhood.

He turned to see if Robert saw what he was seeing, but he was eyeing the collection of bottles behind the bar, arranged in front of a large gilt-framed mirror.

When he turned back, Lacy was no longer there. In fact, at this hour of the afternoon, they had the bar to themselves.

Of course Lacy had never been there, neither her nor her ghost. Perhaps an old memory had simply materialized for a moment, raising its head as Lacy's energy floated about the room. Perhaps it was just wishful thinking.

Jasper decided against saying anything about what he'd seen, or thought he'd seen.

Robert put a hand on Jasper's shoulder and squeezed. "What can I get you?"

Jasper closed his eyes for a moment, smiling. "A cosmopolitan, please." He knew Lacy would approve. It was their signature drink—kind of a tip of the hat to the *Sex and the City* gals.

"Coming right up." Robert moved toward the waiting bartender, a fiftysomething woman with buzzed salt-and-pepper hair and blocky black-framed glasses. She had a copy of the arts section of the *Chicago Tribune* spread out on the counter before her. Candles flickered on the bar, but they didn't hide the smell of her cigarette.

*

They'd each had three drinks. Robert had Johnnie Walker Blue Label, neat. He'd insisted on buying each round, and Jasper didn't object, especially when he learned the cost for Robert's shot was fifty bucks a pop. The thought of spending fifty dollars on a shot of *anything* made Jasper's head swim, yet Robert didn't seem fazed. Besides, that twenty in Jasper's wallet needed to last him until Friday. Jasper had tried to get Robert to drink at least one cosmo, in Lacy's memory, but Robert said he "never mixed."

Emboldened by the liquor now flowing in his veins, Jasper asked Robert, "So tell me why you hadn't seen your niece in so long."

Robert stared down at the table for a moment, then met Jasper's gaze with his own. "Are you trying to make me feel guilty?" He traced an old round water stain with his finger. Then he lifted his head to meet Jasper's gaze once more. "It's a serious question, Jazz."

Jasper caught his breath. No one ever called him Jazz—only Lacy. "No. No, not at all. I'm genuinely curious."

"You don't know who I am, do you?"

"You're Lacy's uncle."

"Yes, but Lacy never mentioned me?"

Jasper shook his head and swallowed the remainder of his drink. "She might have, but not that I remember."

Robert pointed to the empty glass. "Another?"

Jasper put his hand over the top of the glass. "I better not. But thank you." He noticed some initials that had been scratched into the tabletop, EN, and wondered who he or she was. He looked back up. "I'm sorry, but best as I can recall, she never said she had an uncle. But as I also told you, we really didn't talk about family much."

"What *did* you talk about?"

Jasper smiled. "Clothes. What was on Netflix or Hulu. Boys." He raised his eyebrows and Robert laughed. "Boys especially."

"Did Lacy have a fella?"

Without thinking, and maybe because of the drink, Jasper blurted, "Me."

"You?" Robert did a double take. "I thought you were—"

"What?" Jasper cocked his head. "Light in the loafers? Friend of Dorothy? Power bottom?"

Robert cracked up again. "Yes, yes. All of the above." He arched his brows. "Power bottom? Really?"

Jasper felt heat rise to his cheeks. "Well—"

"I thought you were gay. Like me. Oh God, that sounds like an after-school special. Remember those? No. You're too young. But I can just see one called *Gay Like Me*, with Paul Lynde or Charles Nelson Reilly—and you probably don't even know who they are." He shook his head. "I don't know why I said that. Today, they'd definitely cast Sara Gilbert."

"Or Betty White, as Grandma. And a very special guest appearance by Adam Rippon. You know Adam Rippon?" Jasper shook his head. "No, you're too old."

"Hey, watch it."

Jasper forged onward. "Anyway, I think we've established we're both gay. And it seems odd to me that Lacy never mentioned you, given that fact."

"Quit making me feel bad. Why odd, anyway? Just because we're both gay doesn't mean anything."

"Sorry."

"You were the one who said you were her fella, starting all the confusion. Are you...bi or something?"

"Sweetie, power bottoms are never bi. We take an oath when we're sworn in." Jasper rolled his eyes. "But, uh, I think Lacy might have thought of me as her fella, as you say."

"Really? Didn't she know?"

"Oh Jesus, how could she *not* know? No, we *met* in a gay bar. Sidetrack. Down in Boystown. It was show-tunes night, and I knew all the words to 'Send in the Clowns.'" Jasper cast his thoughts back to a warm summer night after a day at the gay beach, sunburned skin, being more than a little drunk, and a goth girl eyeing him from across the bar and laughing. It had been love at first sight.

"She always knew," Jasper said. He stared down at the table for a long time, wishing suddenly that Lacy's passing had all been a dream and she actually *was* sitting at a table across the room, wearing her lace gloves and sipping a cosmo. How could he go on without her? He lifted his gaze to Robert. "I said I was her fella because I know she thought of me that way."

Robert set down his glass and cocked his head.

"In the whole time I knew her, once we became friends, she never dated a guy. We slept together, not in *that* way, but maybe in a way that meant more. She doted on me. And I let her. We never went to a straight bar in hopes of finding someone for her. It was always my choice, and she always seemed happy to hang out with the boys. She never seemed to mind when I'd leave her alone at the bar to go home with some one-nighter. But I think she did.

"She'd always want to know about him the next morning. I'd tell her everything...and I mean *everything*. I couldn't get a blush out of that girl if I tried."

Jasper gave out a little hiccupping sound and began to cry, cursing himself for it. When he could get his breath together enough to speak, he asked, "And do you think I ever asked her about her love life...or want of a love life? Did I ever try to help her find someone? No! Then I wouldn't have my best friend. I wouldn't have my crutch when we went out, a crutch I was willing to throw aside as soon as a pretty boy looked my way. I'm sure she minded sometimes. I was thoughtless. I was selfish. I was inconsiderate. I took her for granted. Until now, when it's too late." Jasper let out a shaky breath, feeling that he'd betrayed her, that her suicide was his fault because he couldn't ever be all she needed and wanted him to be.

"You don't know that," Robert said in an obvious attempt to comfort him.

"Yes, yes, I *do* know that. I knew it when I'd drag my slutty ass in at 3:00 a.m. and she'd be waiting up. She never chastised me or said she'd been worried. No, she'd listen to me pour out the same old story every time—how cute he was at the bar and then he was an asshole at his place. How he used me and then sent me off, because he had to 'get up early.' She'd always be so comforting, so kind. She'd always put a little hope in my bank.

"And we'd almost always end up snuggling in her bed and spooning as we drifted off." Jasper snorted with laughter. "She never even complained about the smells! Alcohol out of my pores and rubbed-off Old Spice!"

Robert chuckled.

"I was the reason she killed herself." *There. It's out. Admitted. Confessed. No turning back.* Jasper thought he might as well think of himself as a murderer. Because if he'd only reciprocated a little where Lacy was concerned, only shown her a fraction of the kindness she'd shown him instead of taking, taking, taking, she might be alive today.

Robert shook his head. He took Jasper's hand in his own, intertwining their fingers and squeezing so hard it hurt a little. "You give yourself too much credit, my friend. Maybe you did play into the reasons my niece decided she didn't want to live anymore, but you can't take it all on your shoulders. For one, it's kind of vain to think that way. I have no doubt you guys loved each other; I can see that in your eyes, in your tears. You grieve, and often when we grieve, we want to blame someone, even if it's ourselves.

"Yeah, you might have made her wish that you were a straight boy and that you held the key to romantic bliss as no one else could, but you also have to give yourself credit for bringing a lot of happiness and security into her life. It sounds like you were great friends. Dare I say soul mates?

"We do what we want to, and Lacy chose to be with you, chose to go out to gay bars with you, chose to have you by her side in bed. Maybe it wasn't ideal, and maybe it was. We'll never know because she can't tell us. But don't beat yourself up. I know the family she came from. I know who her father was and the things that went on when she was growing up..." Robert's voice trailed off, and Jasper wondered if it was because the history he hinted at was dark.

Families always had secrets.

Robert closed his eyes. "And you're gonna make me cry." He swiveled, turning to face the bartender, who was still studying her newspaper.

"Hey!" He laughed. "I'm sorry, what's your name? I don't know you well enough to call you honey or doll."

"Thanks. If you did, you'd know I'm no doll. Anyway, it's Venus. You know, goddess of the mountaintop?"

Robert laughed again. "Sure. Venus is your name. So, Venus, would you mind bringing us just one more round?"

"No problem, sweetie." Venus busied herself mixing and pouring. Jasper met her brown-eyed gaze and saw kindness there. He wondered if she'd overheard their conversation.

She brought the drinks to them. Leaning down, she said softly, "These are on me. Sorry for your loss."

They both thanked her. She hurried off, waving away their gratitude.

Robert lifted his glass. "To Lacy."

Jasper noticed that he used what Jasper thought of as her *real* name, and he appreciated it. "The best friend I'll ever have." Jasper clinked his glass against Robert's.

They didn't talk for a while. Even through the tinted front window, Jasper could see the snow was still coming down. He thought of how Lacy would have loved it. "I'm not one of those Chicago people who bitch and moan about the cold and the snow," she'd say. "I love it."

And she did. On cold snowy days, she'd whip up a batch of her beef stew, which used Guinness as a main ingredient, and the two of them would sit inside, eating big bowls of the stuff with a hunk of beer bread, watching old weepers like *Imitation of Life* and *Madame X*, feeling all safe and warm inside with the steam radiator clanking every so often as though to remind them from where the warmth they enjoyed was coming. She'd also force him to get bundled up so they could have a "day at the beach" as she called it, heading down to the shore at the end of the street. Fargo Avenue beach would be deserted, blanketed in white, with ice creeping out from the shoreline. Those days, she could make him feel like they were the only two people on earth. They'd make snow angels and bombard each other with snowballs, like little kids.

"You're remembering her, aren't you?" Robert asked.

Jasper nodded and took a big gulp of his drink so he wouldn't sob. "How did you know?"

"I could see it in your eyes." Robert touched Jasper's cheek. "And what beautiful eyes they are. At first I thought you had tinted contacts, because they're such a gorgeous emerald color, but they're not, are they? I don't see any sign of contacts."

"Just my eyes, I thank my mom for the color. You're the one, though, with beautiful eyes."

Just then, the door opened, and a trio of guys came in, laughing and stamping snow off their feet. They looked like Loyola frat boys. They were cute, but Jasper resented their intrusion. He was just beginning to feel comfortable and comforted around Robert.

Robert eyed him, and the lines around those fantastic eyes, the creases in his forehead, his close-shorn beard and thinning hair, more salt than pepper, gripped something in Jasper. His full lips, begging to be kissed. One more cosmo and Jasper thought he could easily lean across the table and plant one on him, in full view of Venus and the frat boys, who were now climbing up on stools and clamoring for Leinenkugels.

"How old are you, anyway?" he blurted out. The question came to him from out of nowhere, but he knew deep down he'd been wondering since Robert had first confronted him outside the washroom at the funeral home.

"Just turned fifty," Robert said, with what Jasper perceived as a hint of pride. "How old are you?"

Jasper smiled. "Why, sir, I'm half your age."

Robert nodded. "And next you're gonna say you're young enough to be my son."

"Yuck. No. I wasn't gonna say that because I think you're kind of hot, and I wouldn't want to spoil the moment or the heat I'm feeling right here." Jasper placed a hand over his heart, although the real furnace was firing up much farther south.

"How about 'you look good—for your age'? Is that on the tip of your tongue?"

Jasper shook his head, even though it was. Then he realized the truth: Robert looked good, period.

There was a jukebox in the bar. Even though Jasper rarely saw them anymore, it fit in here at Wishful Drinking, providing a dreamy red-and-yellow luminance to the corner in which it sat. One of the frat boys, a blond who looked like he just stepped out of a J. Crew catalog, wandered over to it.

In only moments, R. Kelly's remix of "Ignition" blared out.

Robert closed his eyes and pursed his lips. "No," he whispered.

Jasper leaned forward. "I hate it too. We should go."

Robert opened his eyes and gave him a pointed look. Jasper wanted to remind him that he had not said something like, "Do you want to get out of here?" which could signal "Let's get somewhere alone together." But he thought Robert might have taken it that way.

And Jasper had to admit that he didn't mind the idea... Robert was much older than guys he usually hooked up with, and if the man had shown up on his Scruff app, Jasper would have immediately discounted him. Honestly, he was indifferent about older men. Like a lot of other guys he knew his age, he simply didn't see them.

And that was sad.

But Jasper was reevaluating what he found attractive. Maybe those guys his age who said they were into DILFs weren't so far off base. Youth had its charms, of course, but age brought wisdom, experience, and, one could hope, control.

But even if Robert was having amorous thoughts, Jasper knew he couldn't do anything sexual with him. At least not today. It would be like betraying Lacy all over again. And even if he thought she might be looking down at the two of them and giving a celestial thumbs-up, Jasper knew, in his heart of hearts, that what he really needed was to be alone.

He wanted suddenly to simply go home and crawl into Lacy's bed, pull up the covers, and immerse himself in her smell. Her pillow would be infused with the aromas of makeup and Chanel No. 5. He wanted to drift off with those smells in his nostrils and then wake later, when it was dark. He'd look out the windows and see the cones of falling snow in the streetlight illumination and think about how she'd made her famous Belgian stew. Maybe he'd even run over to Jewel and get what he needed.

Robert shocked him out of his reverie by handing him his peacoat. "Let's go," he said over the blare of the music.

Jasper shrugged into his coat, pulled his gloves out of the pockets, and put them on. He stood waiting by the door as Robert settled up with Venus. He didn't know the size of the bill he gave her, but the surprise and delight on her face were apparent even from across the room. Her "on the house" round, Jasper figured, had been more than paid for.

She leaned across the bar and gave Robert a hug, which surprised Jasper.

Robert shrugged into his camel-colored coat, cashmere most likely, as he walked toward Jasper.

"Ready?" he asked.

Jasper nodded. *How do I tell him he's not coming home with me? How do I get out of going to his hotel with him (luxurious, probably on the Mag Mile)?* Jasper *tsk*ed himself for being presumptuous.

They headed out.

A wind whipped the still-falling snow almost sideways as they stood under the meager shelter of the bar's burgundy awning. The snow felt like needles in Jasper's face.

Robert pulled his phone out. "I'll call an Uber. Can I drop you off anywhere?" He tapped the screen a few times.

Jasper shook his head. "I live around the corner. I can walk."

"Nonsense. I'll give you a lift."

"No, really. It would be ridiculous and probably out of your way. It'll take me, like, five minutes, if that."

Robert gave him a look that spoke volumes about what he hoped—Jasper knew he was searching for a way to get him alone. Jasper didn't think he was flattering himself. He knew enough about men to know a look when he got one—it was held a little longer than normal.

"Are you sure?" Robert asked.

Jasper wasn't. Yet there was something in his heart yearning for sanctuary, which he could only find on his own. "I kind of want to be by myself now. I think the loss is hitting."

"But won't you be bothered by being there? In the place where she..."

"I like to think of the place where she..." He drew in a shuddering breath. "It's simply the place she *lived* with me. Where we were happy. I thought it might be hard to be there, but her things, her scent, our memories—they're a comfort."

"I understand."

Despite the weather, Jasper looked to the west, where he could see a black SUV making its way through the snow. "I think your ride's almost here."

Robert handed his phone to Jasper. "Put your number in, okay?"

Jasper experienced a little frisson of joy at his request, was more than a little flattered. After removing his gloves, he did as Robert asked. He handed the phone back. "I'd like to see you again, Robert."

Robert looked a little sad as his car drew up to the curb. "I fly back to California tomorrow. But who knows?"

Jasper had second thoughts then about asking him back to the apartment, but his heart told him it was too soon. He knew what would happen.

If something was meant to play out between him and Lacy's uncle, it would.

Robert started toward the car. "I'll call you before I head to the airport in the morning." The driver had gotten out and opened the back door. Robert pulled out his wallet and removed something. He hurried back to Jasper and handed it to him.

Jasper glanced down at the business card.

"This has my email, just in case you want to get in touch that way." Robert grinned. "If you want to make the first move."

Jasper tucked the card into his pocket.

Robert returned to the car and started to get inside. "That's my pen name, by the way," he called out before the driver closed the door. "Don't think I gave you the wrong card."

Jasper started walking north up Greenview, toward home. He didn't think much about the card or the pen-name remark until he got to Fargo, his street. He pulled the card out and glanced down at it.

Michael Blake

"Oh my God," Jasper whispered to himself, and then a burst of almost hysterical laughter escaped him as he started walking again. "Not *the* Michael Blake."

Chapter Five

At home, the first thing Jasper did was pull out his phone and bring up Google. In the search bar he typed "Michael Blake author."

Almost a million hits immediately came up. Lest Jasper had any doubts about whom he'd just shared drinks with, the images of the author washed them away. There he was, in all his salt-and-pepper and pale-eyed glory, looking sexy as hell—on the backs of books, at a premiere of a film version of one of his dark suspense titles (with, Jasper noted, the young Olympian swimmer turned actor Cole Barrett on his arm), at what Jasper guessed was his home, sitting under an arch of bougainvillea with a squat glass of scotch in his hand. There were dozens of images, too, of the books he'd written—their noirish stories given faces of red and black, with grunge lettering and moody photography, full of shadows and staring eyes.

The first hit, naturally, was for the Official Michael Blake Website. Jasper clicked on the link. At the top of the landing page was a gorgeous photo of Robert, or Michael as the world knew him, dressed casually in a white oxford-cloth shirt, navy sports coat, and faded jeans, leaning forward and staring into the camera with those damn soulful and mesmerizing eyes. Beside him were cover images of his two latest books: *Dread* and *Misdemeanor*.

Jasper had read them both when they first came out, on the very phone he held in his now-sweating hand. Even though he was usually strapped, whenever Amazon sent him a notice that a new Michael Blake book was available for preorder, he would always buy it.

He'd been reading Michael Blake since he was a freshman in high school, starting at one of his earliest books, a thriller/ghost story about a rehab facility where a kind-seeming orderly was orchestrating the overdosing of patients he didn't approve of called *The Wisdom to Know the Difference*. Jasper had been hooked from that very first book, especially since Blake had made the daring move of writing the protagonist as a gay teenage crystal-meth addict, struggling to escape his demons and get clean.

Jasper looked up from his phone and cried out, "Why didn't you ever tell me?" as though Lacy were only in the other room. Now it wasn't so much a question of not telling your gay roommate that you had a gay uncle, but telling your compulsive-reader roommate that, in fact, your uncle was one of the most famous writers on the planet, not to mention being one of Jasper's literary heroes.

He listened for a response, but all he got in return was the rumble of the L outside his window. A mechanical voice intoned that Howard would be the next and last stop and that riders could change for the yellow or purple line.

"Didn't you think I'd want to know? Didn't you think I'd go fanboy crazy?"

Jasper glanced down again at the Michael Blake Official Website, taking in the sections for personal appearances, upcoming film and television adaptations, a way to sign up for his newsletter, and, of course, the obligatory links to Twitter, Facebook, and Instagram.

He set the phone down on the coffee table and wandered into Lacy's room, continuing to talk to her. "I just don't get it, Lace. Why wouldn't you tell me your uncle was a bigshot author? One of my favorites? It doesn't make sense."

He plopped down on her bed. He'd made it up after the paramedics had left, and its deep purple comforter with its almost invisible black roses offered up no reply to his queries. He lay back and considered the ceiling.

He supposed she must have had her reasons for not sharing such a vital piece of her family history. Maybe there was bad blood. That made sense, especially since Robert had told him he hadn't seen Lacy in so many years. He put it down to being in California, being busy, but maybe something had happened.

What?

And what business was it of his anyway?

His brush with fame made him vaguely nauseous. It was just weird. Jasper rolled over and stared out at the dusky gray-and-lavender sky, the snow still coming down, but slower and softer now. He didn't think he could have any further contact with Robert. He was too small-town and small potatoes for the "bestselling author." *I'm not worthy! I'm not worthy!* the comic voice shouted in his head. It wasn't so much worthiness—or maybe it was—but what would he even say to someone who might as well have hailed from another planet?

Jasper was the poor son of a welder from a small town in southern Illinois. He grew up in a two-bedroom, one-bath house furnished with thrift-store junk. He had his GED and one year at a vocational school where he'd briefly, for a reason he could no longer fathom, studied to be a massage therapist. He was a clerk in a discount department store. He had an unremarkable past and no future to speak of.

The thought of even talking to a man like Robert Burroughs was now daunting beyond belief. The fact that he'd spent an afternoon with him made Jasper hold his stomach because of the giddy laughter that erupted out of him.

"I should have known," he said softly, maybe to Lacy, maybe simply to the ceiling. Jasper realized that, over the years, he'd seen Michael Blake's picture here and there, in *Entertainment Weekly* or on one of those entertainment news programs Lacy always dissed him for watching.

But a writer wasn't like an actor. People didn't think about their appearance as much. Jasper tried to think of what J.K. Rowling looked like, or Nora Roberts, but he drew blanks in both cases.

Robert hadn't even looked vaguely familiar to him.

Maybe it was the fact that, in person, he looked even better than any of the professional shots of him Jasper had discovered online. Or perhaps it was because no one expects to sit down to afternoon drinks with a *New York Times* bestselling author, whose work was famous around the world.

"Oh fuck, he must be richer than God!" Jasper chuckled. The notion wasn't an enticing one—which surprised Jasper. It was terrifying and made him feel small. His thoughts went back to his and Lacy's last night together, watching the miniseries about Andrew Cunanan, huddled side by side on the couch with their cosmos. Her words to him a little bit later, as they were heading out for the night, came back to him with crystal clarity.

"Old Andrew Cunanan had the right idea. He just had poor, if you'll pardon the pun, execution."

"Oh, you're terrible, Muriel," Jasper said, echoing Toni Collette in a favorite movie of theirs, *Muriel's Wedding.*

"Seriously, though, you should see if you can't find yourself a nice sugar daddy. Someone who will get you out of this shithole—"

"—and into the palace I deserve?"

"Exactly. Why not? Do it right and you can have all your dreams come true and never have to lift a finger. You're good-looking enough, Jazz, and you know it."

He didn't know if he did know it, but the idea had also occurred to him watching the Cunanan movie. If Andrew hadn't been such a fucked-up loon, maybe he'd be doing fine today, sipping a glass of expensive wine while watching the sun set from some fabulous mansion in the tropics or on the Riviera coast.

Jasper laughed out loud. The idea was absurd. But it almost seemed like providence. Had Lacy been thinking about her uncle when she suggested he find a sugar daddy? And if she was, why hadn't she made any effort to introduce Jasper to him? Why not at least mention him, especially when Jasper was deep within the pages of one of his books.

The room had grown dark while he was lost in memory. He struggled out of his clothes and threw them on the floor, then fell asleep faster than he would have imagined possible.

During the night, he woke only once. And when he did, he swore he could feel her lying beside him.

It's just the Chanel No. 5.

*

In the morning, right on schedule as promised, the phone rang. Jasper leaned over the edge of the bed to fish his phone out of his pocket. He pressed the screen to answer and got the phone to his ear just in time.

"I hope I didn't wake you."

Jasper glanced at the area code—760—and shrugged. Still, he was pretty sure who was calling.

"Robert?"

"At your service. And, sweetie, you can call me Rob, okay?"

Jasper sat up in bed and rubbed his eyes. He was tempted to ask, "And not Michael?" but somehow felt weird about that.

The sun streaming in through the mini blinds was super bright, probably on account of reflecting off last night's snowfall. "Where are you, Rob?"

"I'm at O'Hare. I have to head back to California this morning. Work beckons."

If Jasper hadn't been half-awake, he thought he might have not been as forward with what he said next. But he simply couldn't resist. "Why didn't you tell me you were Michael Blake? I'm a huge fan."

There was a moment of silence and then a chuckle. "How huge? Like, in inches?"

"Oh my God," Jasper gasped. He sat up straighter, growing more alert by the second. "I am not talking dirty with Michael Blake."

"Come on, Jasper. Michael Blake is a character, a persona. He's not me."

"Who did I have drinks with yesterday, then?"

"Me, Rob."

"Just an average Joe?" Jasper asked.

Rob laughed. "Average Rob."

Jasper considered calling him Rob, being so chummy, and it made him cover his mouth with his hand to hold back a giddy burst of laughter. It was just too familiar, like calling Lady Gaga "Stef." Or the Queen of England "Liz." He didn't know if he could. And now, with the prompt he'd just been given, Jasper's mind went completely blank.

After several seconds of dead air, Robert or Rob asked, "You still there?"

With surprising eloquence and economy, Jasper said, "Yup."

Rob waited again and Jasper supposed he got disappointed again if he was anticipating, maybe, more words. "Well, I just wanted to call you before heading out to say that, despite the circumstances, I was really glad we had a chance to meet."

"Um, me too."

"You sure? You don't sound like it."

Jasper sighed. "It's just that... It's just that... Honestly?"

"I wouldn't have it any other way."

"Yeah, I'm a little, um, overwhelmed by who you are. I probably seemed like an idiot."

"Why would you say that?" Rob chastened. "You know what? Never mind. I get that. It happens. People buy into the rich-and-famous crap—think I'm something I'm not. This ideal I could never live up to even if I wanted. Which is why I didn't say anything about who I was when we were together. I needed that time, those drinks. I wanted to share my grief with someone who was close to Heather...or Lacy as you call her."

"Lacy was her name. It's what she wanted. It's what she always went by." *You'd know that if you were in touch.*

"I'll remember that. Anyway, please don't feel I'm any different from anyone else. I'm just a regular guy. I sit to pee, just like everyone else."

Jasper snorted. "Okay. But you *are* different. 'Ya are, Blanche, ya are.'"

"Only in the sense that we're all different. We're all unique," Robert said, then added, "just like everyone else."

Another long silence followed. Jasper had to pee now that his regular morning wood had subsided. The urge made his mind even blanker.

"They're boarding in a few minutes. You have my number and my email. Can we talk some more? I like texts and emails myself. I've always been better on paper."

Jasper was tempted to ask him why he wanted to stay in touch, what he saw in Jasper. But he had the good sense to hold the question in and the understanding to know that, if he'd asked it, he would have done himself a disservice.

"Texts are always good."

"It's *the* vehicle for communication for your generation, that's for sure."

"I'll shoot you one later. What time do you get in?"

Rob told him, and they hung up.

Jasper leaned back against the headboard, the nerves in his face singing as if he were a little high.

He smiled.

And then shivered.

After he took care of peeing, he returned to the warmth of Lacy's sheets and her dark comforter, holing up in the slatted sunlight and allowing himself to imagine knowing someone like Rob.

It seemed too fairy tale, too *Pretty Woman* to even believe.

When he scrunched down even farther under the covers, he felt a scrap of paper at the foot of the bed, buried beneath the bedclothes. Thinking it was probably an old receipt or takeout menu, something like that, he managed to snatch the piece of paper with his toes and bring it up to his face.

Jasper let out a gasp that bordered on a scream when he saw what the paper was. It was a note from Lacy.

She began with a snatch of poetry:

The last scud of day holds back for me,
It flings my likeness after the rest, and true as any, on the shadow'd wilds,
It coaxes me to the vapor and the dusk.

I depart as air, I shake my white locks at the runaway sun,
I effuse my flesh in eddies, and drift it in lacy jags.

I bequeathe myself to the dirt to grow from the grass I love,
If you want me again, look for me under your boot-soles.

You will hardly know who I am, or what I mean,
But I shall be good health to you nevertheless,
And filter and fibre your blood.

Failing to fetch me at first, keep encouraged,
Missing me one place, search another,
I stop somewhere, waiting for you.

And then she went on to say,

> *My dear Jazz,*
>
> *I'll start with the old cliché, "If you're reading this, I'm already dead." And I am, huh? Was my funeral nice? What did you wear? More importantly, what did I wear? I hope you didn't allow my mom to dress me.*
>
> *Anyway, I just wanted to say goodbye to you and to apologize. I figure you'll be the one to find me, and I know how hard that will be. I'm crying and having second thoughts as I picture you.*

Jasper held the piece of lined notebook paper away, trying to breathe. "Why didn't you act on those second thoughts, then?" he cried out to the empty room. "You could still be here." Sobbing. "You didn't have to go."

After a moment to calm himself, he read on.

> *I had to go, though. I know you're thinking I left because of you, because you think I pined over you, imagining what we could never have. I'd say "Don't flatter yourself" but there is a kernel of truth to it. You would have made a great husband, except for the fact, as we said many times, you like dick as much as I do.*

Jasper allowed a weak laugh to escape.

> *But really, I needed to go because I couldn't live anymore with the secrets and lies, the ugliness that's my past and my childhood. I'll spare you. It*

won't do any good to drag those shadows out now. Let's just leave it at there was a reason I always wore black and looked like some Anne Rice character.

But those were my scars. And they just wouldn't fade. Many nights, as you snored beside me, I would cry into my pillow. Tears are supposed to be a release, but all mine ever did was remind me of the black hole my life was.

Jazz, I'm almost thirty-three. I'm a shopgirl. I live in a one-bedroom practically on the L tracks— with mice and cockroaches. And you. You're a cut above those critters, rest assured. I assert it on my deathbed. My 'boyfriend' is a handsome, young, kind, smartass, and very vibrant young man who shouldn't be bedding down with me, but instead should be building a fabulous life for himself.

You're free, Jazz. So, and you have to do this because it's my dying wish, so go out there and find someone who cares about you as much as I do, but who can also give you the intimacy and the kind of love you really need and want.

It's okay. I just don't want to go on. I'm good with that.

When you think of me, think of the lines above. I'll leave it to you to figure out who the poet was. Little task for you.

Don't: ever search out what my darkness was. Don't: mourn me too much. I want you to live, to love, to find the real happiness I never could.

Except...a little bit...with you. And we both know, that wasn't quite right.

Bye, Jasper, my only love.

Jasper collapsed back into the pillows, sobbing.

After a while, his nose feeling stuffed, his eyes raw, red, and burning, Jasper forced himself to get out of bed to confront making himself some coffee with the French press. He'd figure things out because now he had no other choice. For now, there was no one to make coffee for him.

He'd left Lacy's note on his own bed, folded neatly. He doubted that he'd share it with anyone, because, really, it was only meant for him. Plus it was solid, concrete proof she'd committed suicide, and he didn't want to take away the shred of hope her parents had that she accidentally overdosed. Let them have that. He didn't know about the secrets and lies she obliquely referred to in her letter, but he was pretty sure they had to do with Mom and Dad.

Did it matter now? What her parents had done or not done as she grew up?

He was a little curious, though, futile as that was. Had Lacy been abused?

Did she witness the kind of horror that I did? Jasper pushed the thought away. No one had witnessed what he had growing up. No one had had a childhood like his, steeped in mystery, horror, tragedy, and loss.

Why, losing Lacy, the one person he truly cared about in the world, was simply par for the course. Jasper's young life had been so filled with trauma, he wondered if there were truly anything else for him out there.

He went into the kitchen. The water in the teakettle was boiling, and the kettle was screaming. He took it off the gas. Lacy always said to heat the water just below the boiling point for the best brew. "If you listen to the kettle, you know when it's getting ready to whistle." He could see her eyes and her smile as they stood together in the kitchen, one of many mornings. "It's kind of like a buildup."

"Like when a guy I'm with is getting close to coming?"

Lacy shrieked with laughter. "Yeah, something like that."

He'd already screwed up the first part of making coffee. He thought he could wait, let the boiling water cool a bit, but he was too impatient. He poured the steaming water into the press and gave the resulting dark brown sludge a stir with a wooden spoon. He set the microwave timer for five minutes.

In the living room, for just a moment, he saw Lacy stretched out on the couch. She eyed him and said, "Next time, wait."

And then, with a blink, he was alone again.

Chapter Six

A lot can happen in a few months.

It was now early spring. In Chicago the snow had melted, leaving the ground damp and the earthy areas soggy. There was an aroma to the air, the smell of change even before buds opened. Wet stones and earthworms. Life.

The temperature had risen—but stubbornly, not much—leaving the air slightly warmer but mitigated by the wet of the thaw and the rain. Even when temperatures were above freezing, you still might feel colder than you had in the winter when it was in the single digits. The wet chill was pervasive.

It was this weather Jasper had described in his last email to Rob. These days almost every morning kicked off with an exchange. Fortunately for Jasper, he didn't have to use his phone this particular day, because his roommate, a silent fellow who worked at a call center out in the suburb of Northbrook, wasn't home. Usually, Stan Thomas worked nights, but yesterday, understaffed, his employer had called him in for a day shift. He was only slightly less noticeable when he was actually gone from the apartment, which, to Jasper, was an invaluable plus in a roommate.

Stan being absent allowed Jasper to hop onto the giant iMac Stan had on the desk in his room (which had once been Lacy's), a room from which he seldom emerged. Stan had all the earmarks of a hermit, including a seeming inability to speak, no friends, a sallow complexion, and the undernourished frame of one Mr. Ichabod Crane. Jasper had no idea what his roomie did in those long, silent hours alone in his room—and didn't dare imagine.

However, Stan paid his rent on time. He didn't ever judge (at least out loud) Jasper for his parade of one-night stands or his affinity for anything rainbow-themed. He was the next best thing to living alone, which Jasper would have loved to do. Rents in a city like Chicago made the prospect of living by himself in his own one-bedroom apartment an impossible dream.

Stan was not, as far as Jasper knew, gay. Jasper didn't know what he was, really. He didn't seem to be straight either. He showed no interest in either sex, no interest in people, really. Perhaps he was "ace," or asexual. Jasper had heard the term bandied about online, but with his own raging libido, found the existence of such people hard to imagine, like unicorns or leprechauns.

Stan was as quiet and unobtrusive as an elderly cat. And that suited Jasper just fine, especially when he was out of the house and Jasper could commandeer his desktop computer with its twenty-seven-inch screen. For one thing, PornHub looked *so* much better there than on his phone.

But that was beside the point. It was nice to be able to read and respond to Rob's emails on a screen where he could often take in the whole missive without having to scroll. And when Jasper wrote, the words simply appeared more *real* on the big Retina display. They even seemed to flow better.

He still had yet to shake the surreal feeling, even after many, many email and text exchanges, that he was actually corresponding with *the* Michael Blake.

He and Rob had been writing back and forth now for a couple of months. Jasper had gotten to know the man behind many of his favorite books so much better but had yet to uncover any of the "secrets and lies" Lacy had alluded to in her suicide note.

Jasper wondered if he really needed to know about those. He'd gotten over his initial trepidation about Rob being so much older and richer. Despite things being surreal, he'd even stopped being a fanboy and could view Rob as a real friend, someone he wanted to know better.

Emails, Jasper thought, allowed both of them to open up without fear or hesitation. Rob had confessed early on that he despised talking on the phone because his mind often went blank and the pressure of that open line often left him feeling vulnerable and witless.

Jasper felt the same. So they wrote. And they talked...and grew in intimacy, without the pressure of physical proximity, which brought its own Pandora's box full of miseries and delights.

For example, Jasper had learned five things, among others, about Rob that surprised him and piqued his interest:

1. He'd been married very briefly to a model—whose name, even today, would be familiar to most—when he was in his late teens. The marriage had lasted for less than one week and had ignited a flurry of tabloid interest.

2. He got his first agent by pestering Stephen King's until the beleaguered agent connected him with an upstart in Brooklyn who sold Michael Blake's first book. The rest was history, and that Brooklyn professional

would forever thank Stephen King's agent for making her rich.

3. He loved three things—morning runs, coffee, and his dog, Kodi, a Chihuahua/Shiba Inu mix he'd rescued from the Palm Springs Animal Shelter. When Rob took him on, he'd had a long record of biting and debilitating shyness, both induced by extreme fear, the details of which would forever remain unknown. He'd been discovered wandering on a street near the airport, emaciated and infested with fleas. No one knew his exact age or what caused him to cower at the simple nearness of a human hand. "I took him on," Rob explained in one email, "because I saw myself in him."

4. Perhaps not surprisingly, Rob had had very few romantic relationships, even though he was embarking on his sixth decade on the planet. "I've just never clicked with anyone," he wrote. "Never?" Jasper had asked. And he'd responded, "It's my deepest, darkest secret (well, one of them anyway) that I've never been in love. I don't even know what it feels like. Maybe I'm just not capable." Jasper had done research online and had seen Rob, aka Michael Blake, the openly gay suspense author, paired up with high-level businessmen, actors, athletes, and even a politician (Democrat, thank God), but Rob explained all of them were, more or less, for "publicity purposes," and the images Jasper'd seen on Google were almost all "photo ops" set up by the woman who did his public relations out of her West Hollywood office.

5. He'd lived in Palm Springs for the past fifteen years. "I love the desert. I even love the summer heat. The endless blue skies, the foliage, the kind of weird vibe that comes off the mountains all around us makes me feel at home."

*

Jasper had been stunned, especially, by the revelation that Rob had never been in love. How could that be when Jasper himself had been "in love" more times than he could count? A hairy chest, a sweet lopsided smile, a stubbled face, or even a kind word were enough to convince Jasper he was in love and had found a soul mate. That he tired quickly of these "soul mates," or they of him, didn't mean they weren't in love, only that love was fleeting, and no one knew, really, the answer to the age-old question: How does one make love stay? Yet deep down he knew that Rob's never having been in love was common ground Jasper shared with him.

Jasper revealed to Rob five things about himself, keeping his own tragic and twisted story secret lest he inspire too much pity.

1. He'd never owned a pet. His dad had always said anything else living—even a goldfish—was too much for him to take care of. With Jasper, he was burdened enough. One mouth to feed was more than adequate, thank you very much. "Feeding me was the least my dad could do—and he rose spectacularly to that level," Jasper wrote. He'd always wanted a dog or a cat but had never found the time to care for one. And if there was one lesson he learned from his wounded, damaged, and damaging father, it was that if you don't have the time and attention to give to another living thing, then leave it alone.

2. Despite feeling comfortable that his dad was distant, hard to love, and nearly impossible to get close to, and despite his being Jasper's own, and only, flesh and blood, he still longed to have a relationship with the man. "Someone once told me I could only do that if I accepted

him as simply a fellow human being, flawed as he was, and *not* a parent. That made logical sense to me, but I don't know if I can ever internalize it." Without going into detail about his past, Jasper had confided in Rob that he "understood why his dad was the way he was. He'd been so hurt as a young man, so traumatized, that he probably suffered from some form of PTSD that was never treated."

3. Although Jasper had loved many men in his own way (and he begrudgingly admitted he may have been confusing lust with love), he'd never thought he, himself, was much of a catch. "I'm too skinny. My nose is too big. I snore. I'm uncoordinated. I have no social graces whatsoever. I'm selfish..." was just the beginning of a laundry list of flaws Jasper perceived within himself. Rob wrote back that Jasper's flaws were imagined. "You're undoubtedly one of the most beautiful men I've ever laid eyes on, and the fact that you don't seem to realize it makes you even more beautiful." Jasper thought Rob was full of it, but even knowing that, he'd walked on a cloud all day after getting that message.

4. He loved old movies, especially old tearjerkers. "The more I cry, the higher the movie's star rating." He sent Rob a list that included: *Written on the Wind; Imitation of Life; Stella Dallas; Charly; Goodbye, Mr. Chips; Longtime Companion; Philadelphia; Steel Magnolias; Brief Encounter; Old Yeller; Ghost; Brian's Song; E.T.; Brokeback Mountain; It's a Wonderful Life*; and of course *The Wizard of Oz.*

5. He'd never been west of the Mississippi. "I'd love to travel, but who can afford it?" he'd wondered, knowing Rob could. What must it be like, Jasper speculated, to be able to jet off to anywhere one's heart desired? First class? When he thought of his meager paycheck, he realized he

might have to accept the fact that it was possible he'd never know.

*

At first, Jasper was uncomfortable with the email-only arrangement, but then he found some patience. He discovered he enjoyed getting to know a man's heart and brain before what his dick felt like inside him.

Not that he didn't fantasize about the latter!

Today he didn't need to be in at the store until early afternoon. Now he was seated at Stan's desk, the brushed-aluminum desk lamp banishing the dark of the morning outside, a cup of Starbucks dark-roast French-press coffee steaming in a mug beneath the glow of the lamp. He'd become a master at making coffee and, at times, comforted himself that Lacy was guiding his hand as he made his first attempts at getting the grind right, the temperature perfect, and the steeping time down.

And he realized, with the rain pouring outside and the distant rumble of thunder, that he at last felt comfortable here in Lacy's old room. Even though Stan lived here and had moved in his own Ikea furniture, it would always be Lacy's room in Jasper's mind. For a long time after she died, he'd find himself tearing up simply standing in the doorway, remembering.

But with time came acceptance. And now he could remember the room fondly, with memories of sleeping cuddled up with her something to be grateful for rather than something to despair of. The memories were becoming more soft caresses than pinpricks to his heart.

She'd stopped appearing to him too. Those instances may or may not have been his imagination, but he treasured them whatever they were. Yet he didn't feel sad when he noticed they were gone. Their absence must mean Lacy had moved on to whatever realm she now occupied. And that made him happy.

Perhaps the happiness she sought was beyond the veil.

It also allowed Jasper to move on somewhat too. He'd never have imagined he could feel comfortable, almost cozy, in this room. But he did.

He clicked on the Chrome browser icon in the toolbar at the bottom of the iMac's screen to open it, then brought up Gmail and entered his username and password.

An email from Rob (Michael Blake! Michael Blake is writing to me personally! On an almost daily basis!) always made him smile and gave him a serious jolt of pleasure.

There was one waiting. He clicked on it and began reading.

> *One of the things I've learned as a writer is to come right to the point. Forego distraction. Worship brevity, clarity, and simplicity.*
>
> *So, I'll jump right in.*
>
> *I want to see you. No, not a picture of you (although some of the ones you've sent have been very nice—and some have even made my temperature, along with other things, rise).*
>
> *You. In the flesh. What a lovely turn of phrase.*
>
> *I know you've never been to Palm Springs. Never been to California, even. Or, as you've often lamented, never even west of the Mississippi.*
>
> *Would you be willing to deepen our email canoodling with an in-person visit?*

Jasper stopped reading then because he felt sick. For one, he had no money to make this man's dream come true. Literally no money. Once he paid his half of the rent and utilities, bought meager food from Aldi, and allowed himself a few cocktails here and there around Chicago, he had nothing left over. Nada.

For another, he'd gotten comfortable with this arrangement and wasn't even sure he wanted more. He'd fantasize sometimes, of course, about being swept off his feet ala *Pretty Woman*, but the truth was, if he thought about his own romantic future, the most he dared hope for was that he'd meet a hunky fireman from the South Side, or maybe a swarthy Italian chef from Wicker Park, or even a cute boy who worked in retail like him and they'd pool their resources eventually to get their own studio apartment and puppy or kitten together. They'd vacation in Saugatuck or at the Dells. Their cars would always be secondhand. But who cared? They'd have each other.

The idea of being involved in any way with someone rich and famous like Rob was almost absurd. It certainly was surreal.

He drank his tepid coffee and got up to go to the kitchen to refill his cup. There, he opened the back door and stepped onto the landing to look out over the building's backyard, which was bordered on one side by a large retaining wall above which perched the L tracks.

Rain sheeted down. The landscape seemed sodden, as though waterlogged. The sky was a dark gray—so dark, in fact, it was pretty close to being indistinguishable from night. A train huffed on the tracks across from him, and he wondered if anyone could see him, standing here shivering in a Steppenwolf Theatre Company T-shirt and plaid boxers, clutching a chipped Human Rights

Campaign mug. Wondered if he was seen and judged a cliché.

He laughed and went back inside about the time his teeth were ready to start chattering.

He started reading the email again, and it was almost as though Rob could see him.

> *Sunshine! I have Chicago on my phone's weather app and I know what it's like there now. Highs in the low forties, lows in the twenties. Dreary, rainy skies, worthy of London or Seattle.*

> *Here it's sunny every single day. By midafternoon, we hit the eighties and it cools down at night to the fifties or sixties, perfect for soaking in my hot tub with a glass of wine and staring up at the stars, which are not, unlike Chicago, drowned out by light pollution. Imagine a sky crowded with stars. You can see the constellations. Here's some poetry I love about stars and I think of it often when I look up at night, dreaming:*

They are immortal, all those stars both silvery and golden shall shine out again,

The great stars and the little ones shall shine out again, they endure,

The vast immortal suns and the long-enduring pensive moons shall again shine.

> *I'll leave it to you to figure out the poem and the poet.*

> *Come see the stars from my backyard, which backs up to the mountains. Come feel the desert air caress you.*

I tire of these emails. Will you come? Say the word and a first-class ticket to Palm Springs will be waiting for you at O'Hare. You don't even need to pack (grin). Just be here.

And Rob ended it there.

I won't have to pay. The thought both comforted and repelled. Jasper had learned long ago to stand on his own two feet, that taking anything from anyone was charity—pitiable. Plenty of his bar friends, he knew, would jump at a chance like this, not thinking twice about it, just taking.

But he had his pride.

Still, it *was* tempting. He rose once more from the desk and moved to the balcony off the living room, where he could survey Fargo Avenue from his second-story vantage.

The rain had slowed to a sprinkle, maybe even a fine mist. But the skies were still dark enough for the streetlights to remain on. Every few seconds a low grumble in the background reminded him the day's rain was far from over. The hiss on the pavement could move in an instant to drumming.

A chill wind, too cold for spring, blew up from the east, making Jasper shiver. He wrapped his arms around himself. "Get back inside, idiot. Don't you have sense enough to come in out of the rain?"

He thought of clear, sunny skies. The heat of that yellow orb beating down, warming, loosening his limbs. Thought of kicking back and napping in that warm embrace.

Pictured a Van Gogh starry, starry night.

Why not take something for once? Why not simply be open to receiving a gift, especially one that could lead to significant change?

He shook his head and moved to the door.

Back inside, he woke the computer and read Rob's email over again. Using the mouse, he highlighted the snippet of poetry Rob had shared and then plugged it into Google.

Jasper gasped when he saw who wrote the poem. It was called "On the Beach at Night," and the full poem read:

> *On the beach at night,*
>
> *Stands a child with her father,*
>
> *Watching the east, the autumn sky.*
>
>
> *Up through the darkness,*
>
> *While ravening clouds, the burial clouds, in black masses spreading,*
>
> *Lower sullen and fast athwart and down the sky,*
>
> *Amid a transparent clear belt of ether yet left in the east,*
>
> *Ascends large and calm the lord-star Jupiter,*
>
> *And nigh at hand, only a very little above,*
>
> *Swim the delicate sisters the Pleiades.*
>
>
> *From the beach the child holding the hand of her father,*
>
> *Those burial-clouds that lower victorious soon to devour all,*
>
> *Watching, silently weeps.*

Weep not, child,

Weep not, my darling,

With these kisses let me remove your tears,

The ravening clouds shall not long be victorious,

They shall not long possess the sky, they devour the stars only in apparition,

Jupiter shall emerge, be patient, watch again another night, the Pleiades shall emerge,

They are immortal, all those stars both silvery and golden shall shine out again,

The great stars and the little ones shall shine out again, they endure,

The vast immortal suns and the long-enduring pensive moons shall again shine.

Then dearest child mournest thou only for Jupiter?

Considerest thou alone the burial of the stars?

Something there is,

(With my lips soothing thee, adding I whisper,

I give thee the first suggestion, the problem and indirection,)

Something there is more immortal even than the stars,

(Many the burials, many the days and nights, passing away,)

Something that shall endure longer even than lustrous Jupiter

Longer than sun or any revolving satellite,

Or the radiant sisters the Pleiades.

Was it a sign? Lacy's final missive to him had also quoted Walt Whitman. It was too much of a coincidence, he thought, to be anything but. Besides, hadn't he read somewhere that the real meaning of the word coincidence was tied up in synchronicity? He'd also heard once that coincidences weren't as rare an occurrence as some thought.

Coincidence? Omen? Sign?

Jasper knew he needed to follow a sign that suggested there was something "more immortal even than the stars."

He brought up Rob's email, hit Reply, and wrote, *I'll come. Just tell me what my next steps are. I can get a week off starting the end of April.*

He didn't know what else to write. So he hit Send. And immediately began gnawing his nails, regretting it. "You're being a whore, a cheap whore," he told himself, laughing a little hysterically and not all that amused.

*

He was about to get up from Stan's desk when Rob's reply hit. "Jesus, how did you even have time to read, let alone write a response?" he asked the screen, as though it were a magic mirror, one that could see into Rob's soul.

Like the invitation, Rob's reply was short and to the point.

Let me know what dates in April work for you. I'm open all month. No pressing engagements or travel. And it's great you'll get here before the summer heat starts to set in—it's not for the faint of heart!

Once I have a firm date (Oh, the images that conjures up!), I'll get your ticket booked.

And Jasper, please don't feel this obligates you in any way, shape, or form. This is a gift, freely given, that I think will benefit me as much as it does you. So please— no mention of paying me back, in whatever currency you're thinking.

I have no agenda for this trip— I just want to see you again.

Jasper shut his eyes as a smile crept across his face. He thought, oddly enough, of a line from one of his favorite movies, *Rosemary's Baby*. It went something like "This isn't a dream. This is really happening."

He wrote back and told Rob that the last week in April would work great.

Why delay?

Chapter Seven

On the morning he was scheduled to fly out to Palm Springs International Airport, Jasper awoke from barely remembered dreams, the sound of rain hitting hard against his window. He had this vague, gut-twisting feeling of dread. Sweat dampened the pillow beneath his head.

And for just a second, he thought he could smell Old Spice on his pillowcase.

"What the hell?" He turned and sniffed the in-need-of-washing case deeply. Scents of his hair gel and a little sweat maybe rose up, but Old Spice? He wouldn't be caught dead dousing himself with that, not only because it was drugstore stuff, smelly water as cheap as they come, but because Old Spice, especially on a pillowcase, reminded Jasper of his father.

When Jasper was a little boy, he'd often slide into his father's queen-size bed on early weekend mornings when Dad left to go downstairs to make them a typical weekend breakfast—bacon cooked up in the old cast-iron skillet and then eggs fried in the grease. If it was summertime, he'd slice a tomato or two from his garden to accompany the bacon and eggs.

They'd eat while Dad read the paper and Jasper watched him, hoping for a word or two.

Those breakfasts were one of the few happy memories Jasper had of his childhood.

So was the smell of Old Spice on a still-warm pillowcase. For some reason, it made the little boy Jasper feel secure, safe—and those feelings were precious in the Warren household. The warm pillowcase and the scent were like a longed-for embrace.

Now, he couldn't imagine why he'd awaken on this important morning reminded of the smell of his father on a pillowcase.

Unless it was the dream he was having upon awakening?

Fractured images came to him. Blood on an old plaid couch. A pair of upholstery shears on a dirty floor. A grainy newspaper photo showing a crowd gathered outside Thomas's Used Furniture on Sixth Avenue in downtown Haddonfield, Illinois, Jasper's hometown.

That newspaper image chilled him. He knew why. It haunted him to this day. It wasn't just a story in a small-town rag; it was the destruction of his family.

He sat up, stomach grumbling, head pounding.

Even though he couldn't remember much more about the dream, he *could* remember what inspired it.

When Jasper was seven years old, his pregnant mother, Mo, short for Maureen, and his baby sister, Sara, were brutally murdered in that used-furniture store one sweltering August afternoon, along with the proprietor, an older man with the comical name of Dick Popp. All three had been stabbed to death with a pair of upholstery shears. The store's cash register and safe had been emptied. The day had been hot, with temperatures in the nineties and humidity to match. Not many people were out and about, but his mom had been, hoping to find a decent used baby carriage for cheap. People always said she was in "the wrong place at the wrong time" as no one in their little town would have a motive for slaughtering a sweet, young, and pregnant mother and her little girl. It nearly defied belief.

No one had seen or heard a thing. Later, there were a couple of reports of two men running down an alley behind the store. That was it as far as the culprits were concerned. As time went on, the descriptions of the men became more fanciful—there were bloodstains on their clothes; they were high on drugs; they were Satanists, cannibals, escapees from a lunatic asylum; they were white, black, Hispanic...

When he got older, Jasper would come to visit that alley one day to examine its brick surface, with weeds sprouting from the mortar, futilely hoping against hope that a clue might remain. He tried to imagine the killers. Did they feel remorse? Who could do such a thing?

Ultimately, no one was ever caught for the tragic and horrifying crime, although to this day, theories and gossip surrounding the crime still floated around the small town. It was a good spooky story to tell around a campfire. Some believed the murderers were still at large. Some said they were dead. Others attributed many, many unsolved crimes over the years to whomever had snuffed out the lives of Jasper's family.

Except it wasn't just a story for Jasper and his dad. The crime, which had probably taken only minutes to perpetrate, echoed through their years together, marring their very lives with an ugly rust-colored stain.

That summer day it was as though Dad had died too. Jasper had vague recollections so Americana in nature that Jasper wondered if he'd conjured them up out of whole cloth in a need for—what? Closeness? Attention? But he liked to imagine he could remember being a little boy and balancing on his father's shoulders as they watched Fourth of July fireworks at a local park. Maybe there *was* a time when he and his dad tossed a Frisbee back and forth under a summer sky of endless blue. He *thought* he recalled going hunting with his dad one autumn morning, the air crisp and cold, their yellow, red, and black beagle, Topper, his bark sounding like a yodel, pursuing a rabbit through the brush.

Jasper had cried when Daddy shot the rabbit.

Those memories *could have* been real, Jasper thought. They *seemed* authentic enough.

They also could have been someone else's recollections or even scenes from an old movie. Sometimes we want something to be true so much, we imagine it to be so.

What he really remembered for sure was growing up in a two-bedroom, green-shingled house with a man who hardly ever spoke, who took no interest in him. His best vision of his dad was him seated at the maple kitchen table, the daily newspaper spread out before him, a cup of coffee at his side, and a cigarette burning in an ashtray next to that. He never mentioned what was in the news. In fact, beyond what was necessary for school and the like, they seldom spoke. Sadly, this came to feel like a familial norm for Jasper.

It wasn't personal, Jasper always told himself. When Jasper's mom, sister, and unborn sibling had been murdered that day, his father had become a ghost. He went through life as though on automatic pilot. He never seemed to regain any semblance of life, so he went through the motions without feeling anything, a kind of zombie.

To his father's credit, Jasper could claim he'd always been fed and clothed properly. His dad met all the minimum standards for care—Jasper was never hungry or cold.

Except for love. Except for the warmth of love.

Now he sat up in bed and put his feet on the hardwood floor. "Why am I dredging this crap up now of all times?" He hopped from the bed and headed toward the bathroom. "I have a flight to catch."

As he made his way, he heard his phone's ringtone and hurried back to his bedroom. He snatched it off the nightstand where he'd left it the night before to charge.

The caller ID chilled him with its one word: Dad.

Jasper let it go to voicemail.

*

Jasper had never flown before.

At first he froze when the entrance doors under the Alaska sign glided silently open. He couldn't force himself to step inside—deer frozen in the headlights and all that. All the people in the terminal rushing about, the long lines, the sound of nonstop announcements over invisible speakers, and the digital boards, mounted high, posting dozens and dozens of arrivals and departures, overwhelmed him and made beads of sweat break out on his forehead and the palms of his hands.

What do I do? What do I do? How do people know what to do?

He backed up a few steps and ran into a guy about his own age rushing inside.

"Watch it, bud!" the guy exclaimed and veered around Jasper. "Jesus!"

The guy looked like *he* knew what he was doing in his crisp designer jeans, pink oxford-cloth shirt, and leather TUMI bag. He wasn't much older than Jasper, but Jasper felt a world apart.

People know this stuff. Most people anyway. They know how to check a bag. They know what line to get into. What do I do first? Jasper wondered. *Get in one of the long lines? But which one? If I get in the wrong one and wait too long, maybe I'll miss my flight.* Good thing he didn't need to check his nylon duffel bag. He saw people printing out tags for their luggage and had no idea how he would manage *that*. He looked at the threadbare bag, sitting on its wheels beside him, and felt a wave of embarrassment. Rob's luggage was probably all leather, Vuitton or some other designer label.

And speaking of Rob, he most likely knew exactly what to do when he got to the airport. This would be second nature for Rob. He probably had an assistant to take care of all the details and would blithely board the plane when the time came. He'd stroll right on up to that line to Jasper's left, the one that said First Class.

Wait a minute. I'm first class. Rob had told him that his ticket would be waiting at the first-class counter.

He breathed a sigh of relief and got in the first-class line with the other travelers. Thankfully, this line was very short. Yet he immediately felt out of place, as though he were an imposter who had snuck into the grounds of some exclusive enclave. He wouldn't have been surprised if some dark-suited man or woman glided up to him, tapped him on the shoulder, and in a soft voice told him, "You don't belong, sir. You simply do not belong. Please exit the airport now."

But no one did, and Jasper moved forward behind a blonde in yoga pants cradling a Yorkshire terrier in her arms. Her luggage was hot pink. The dog eyed him with what Jasper thought was disdain. Even a Yorkshire terrier found him out of place.

Jasper was sweating by the time his turn came. When he got to the attendant, an older man with a shaved head, gray beard, and cool round red glasses, he was tongue-tied.

The man cocked his head. "ID? Ticket?"

Jasper didn't know what to say. He didn't have a ticket. He just knew he'd be sent away, laughed out of O'Hare for the rube he was.

"Uh, I don't have a ticket."

The man looked at him strangely, and Jasper didn't blame him for his confusion. People waited behind him, and heat rose in his cheeks.

Jasper hastened to add, "There's supposed to be a ticket left for me here? Jasper? Jasper Warren?"

The man chuckled. "Are you asking me your name?"

"No. No, of course not." He remembered then that the man had requested ID. That, he could manage. He groped for his wallet, pulled it from his jeans back pocket, plucked his driver's license out, and set it on the counter.

The guy eyed it, set it down, and then began keying letters into the terminal in front of him. "Ah. Right here, Mr. Warren. Flying to Palm Springs?"

Jasper nodded.

"We have you in the second row, window. I'll print out your boarding pass. Do you want to check your bag?"

Jasper had heard that checking a bag cost extra. "Um, no, that's okay."

The attendant smiled. "It's complimentary, sir."

Finally, Jasper was able to manage a smile in return. "Is it that obvious?" He meant his poverty, his lack of sophistication.

"First time flying?"

"Yeah."

"It can be a bit overwhelming. Just set your bag on the scale here, and I'll check it through to California for you. Then you won't have to worry." He printed out a label for the bag and applied it to its nylon handles. "You'll want to fill out an identification tag with your numbers."

"Sure." Jasper got busy.

The attendant handed him his pass and directed him to security. "After that, you can wait in the Alaska lounge. It'll be on your left after you come out of security. You have plenty of time. Then you proceed to Gate F. You won't need the shuttle, and because you're in first, you're among the first to board. Easy-peasy." He gave Jasper a warm smile and a flash of dark brown eyes. "You don't have to worry about a thing. Relax."

Jasper thanked him, thinking, *At least not until I'm on the ground.*

*

As they neared Palm Springs, Jasper sucked in a breath at the desert landscape and mountains below him. The sky was electric blue and the mountains and desert were unlike anything he'd ever seen. It almost looked like how he'd imagine the surface of Mars would appear. Was there really life down there? It was stunningly, breathtakingly beautiful, but it looked so, so...sterile, almost uninhabitable. The jagged mountains soared into the sky, claiming their space in the neon blue, looking unreal—blue, gray, and a dusty color Jasper couldn't name.

As they neared civilization and descended farther, Jasper began to see signs of life: roads, patches of green (many, many golf courses), even a water park. Most of the buildings and houses seemed low to the ground and bleached by the sun. Red tile roofs dotted the landscape like decorations.

It wasn't long before they were touching down on the runway, and Jasper held fast to his armrests. The three Bloody Marys he'd drunk on the way didn't lessen his anxiety. Touchdown seemed so hard! And his ears hadn't popped, so in the air was true hushed expectancy. He could barely hear the announcements, but everyone stood quickly, whipping out their phones. Heads lowered to screens. Fingers began keying in texts.

Before he knew it, he was headed for the exit. He smiled at the cute flight attendant who mouthed the words "bu-bye" as Jasper stepped off the plane.

Once outside the terminal, Jasper felt he'd traveled to another world, another time, another season. Most of the airport was outdoors, shielded from the sun by giant white tenting. He noticed the terminal was named after Sonny Bono and emitted a burst of laughter. He vaguely remembered seeing an old cassette of his mom's somewhere around the house, *The Best of Sonny and Cher*.

His thoughts of Mr. Bono, whom he knew next to nothing about, were quickly replaced by the scenery. The tall, spindly palms swayed gently in a heated breeze, their fronds glistening green in the sun. And the sun! That ball of fire seemed hotter than it ever had in Illinois, already baking the top of his head, his face, his shoulders.

Other than in movies, Jasper had never seen a palm tree before.

He paused to simply stand at the bottom of the escalator to take in the famous dry heat and the mountains and hills, ochre brown, all around.

He felt like a rube. This, he thought, was truly a pinch-me moment. He had to force himself to go on inside to baggage claim.

*

Once he claimed his bag, he headed outside to wait for Rob, who said he'd pick him up. As they'd agreed, Jasper texted when he landed—with a shaking hand. He felt a little sick now that he was here.

Oh my God, he thought, *what the hell have I done?* He honestly wished he hadn't come. *This is ridiculous. I don't even know the man other than a little conversation over drinks.* He came back with *You've read every single one of his books. You know him. You lived with, and loved, his niece. You know him. You've been writing back and forth for months. You know him. And, there's that little attraction pull the two of you seem to have going on.*

Outside, the sun made Jasper sweat. It wasn't that hot, only in the eighties and virtually no humidity, but that sun! Oh, it was relentless. Jasper had tried to look nice too. From the Rack, he'd picked up a cool Ben Sherman short-sleeve shirt—geometric blue and black shapes on a white background—that fitted him as though tailor-made. Now it was dark under the pits.

Rob hadn't said what kind of car he'd be driving, so Jasper tried to keep his mind off the plusses and minuses of his appearance by scanning every driver and vehicle as it passed by. He wasn't even sure he'd remember what

Rob looked like, despite having pored over pictures of him, both online and sent via their email exchanges.

What kind of car would he drive anyway? Something expensive to be sure. A BMW? Mercedes? Lexus? Something even more exotic? Would he go for a new or maybe a vintage car to match the midcentury vibe of Palm Springs?

Jasper stepped back and away from the curb when he at last saw Rob. He lingered there in the relatively cool shadows, not sure if he could do it, if he could actually go through the visit as though this were a normal thing for him. He had a strong urge to simply turn and run back into the terminal, to lose himself among the vacationing throngs. Maybe he could check in again and head straight back to Chicago where he belonged. He wasn't up to this!

Yet he stood only a few paces away from where he'd originally stood. Rob was back in the long line of cars picking up people, but he was unmistakable, driving what had to be an antique, but perfectly preserved, vehicle. The car was a little two-seater, a shade somewhere between maroon and red, with chrome accents. The top, of course, was down. Even from where he stood, he could see Rob's silver hair and the fine planes of his face, partially hidden by a pair of Ray Bans.

He looked like a movie star. He looked like he so, so belonged here.

And Jasper so, so didn't.

But you're here now, so just make the best of things, for God's sake! He'd survived his first plane trip. He'd traveled a couple thousand miles. The plans were all in place. There was no turning back. *Relax! Try to have a little fun!*

And his man was *here*. In a glorious convertible. And he was coming closer.

Jesus! Get ahold of yourself. Jasper stepped forward, back to the curb's edge. He felt as though his toes were at the end of a cliff. He glanced down at his bag, and his face went supernova—not from the sun, but from shame. It was patched with duct tape, for Christ's sake!

It all happened too fast. Suddenly, there Rob was, pulling up and smiling as though he'd just stepped off a movie screen.

Jasper returned the smile, squinting a bit into the sun.

Rob hopped out of the car to help him put his bag in the trunk. The sight of him took Jasper's breath away. He was taller than Jasper remembered, broader-shouldered. His hair was an almost shimmering silver; Jasper wondered if it had once been black. Unlike the clean-shaven face Jasper had seen when he'd first met him, he now sported a goatee, silver with flecks of black. His ruddy skin was dotted with stubble that Jasper could imagine rubbing against his own clean-shaven face, the delightful sandpaper scratch.

He wore a pair of khaki shorts, a simple white cotton tank top, and leather flip-flops. Palm Springs casual, Jasper guessed. The watch on his wrist, though, looked like a Rolex.

Should I hug him? Shake hands? Jasper had yet to speak.

Rob settled things for him, grabbing him and pulling him tightly into his arms. He whispered, "I'm so glad you're here." Then he moved around the back of the car to hop in the driver's seat.

Jasper got in the passenger side. Still, his mind was a total blank.

Rob revved the engine a little as he put the car in gear, and they sped off. In no time they were on Tahquitz, heading toward a huge mountain range. Tall, spindly palms lined the center of the road. The mountain rose up, huge, so close it seemed they'd run into it.

I'm really here in Southern California.

Jasper put on his sunglasses, trying to pretend this was all nothing special when in fact he felt like an extra in a movie. Finally, when he could get his tongue, lips, and teeth working together well enough to form words, he asked, "So what's the car?"

"It's my baby," Rob said, patting the leather steering wheel. "It's a 1961 Maserati 3500 Spyder. Cool, huh?"

"Restore it yourself?" Jasper asked.

"Ha! I wouldn't trust myself to change the oil. No, I have a guy out in Yucca Valley who's obviously not only a stickler for details but a true artist. Right? What do you drive?"

Jasper didn't answer, but simply stared out the window at some statuary of Mexican workers in the middle of the road. How could he say that the L was what he drove?

*

"I thought you might like to go for a swim before dinner," Rob said as he set two brightly colored beach towels on the bench by the sliding glass doors. "A swimsuit is, of course, optional. But do what makes you the most comfortable. If you forgot yours, just check the outside bath adjacent to the deep end of the pool. It has an assortment of Speedos and board shorts and everything in between in just about any size, color, and pattern you can imagine. But if you prefer au naturel, go for it. No one can see you." He winked because in the air hung the knowledge that "no one" did *not* include Rob. "Except me. And I make no promises not to peek."

Alone now, after a tour of the house, Jasper sat on the bed of the guest room Rob had said was his for the long weekend. Jasper felt a mixture of relief and disappointment at learning that he was *not* expected to stay in Rob's room, in his massive California king-size bed with its soaring reclaimed-wood headboard.

But the man was a gentleman, right? He'd made it clear long before Jasper boarded the plane to come out here that he had no expectations—that this trip was simply a way for two people to get to know each other. Whether the outcome of that further, in-person knowing was a dalliance, a friendship, or something longer and more significant was up to fate, to their hearts' reaction to the other.

No pressure.

And yet Jasper, sitting here on his own bed in a room that had sliding glass doors onto a patio with a sparkling turquoise kidney-shaped pool, felt a little rejected. He guessed his feelings were rooted in clichéd expectations that an older man and a younger man holed up in a house alone together was the perfect setup for the decrepit lech to try to get his hands on the unspoiled, fresh-as-a-spring-peach younger man's flesh.

But it wasn't like that. Not at all. For one thing, Jasper's flesh could just possibly be even more "spoiled" (in a manner of speaking) than Rob's. Jasper had been around the block a time or two. He was no Mary Poppins, as Lacy might have said, a wicked grin lighting up her features. "Honey, if you showed everything that had been stuck into you, you'd look like a porcupine!" Jasper shook his head. Her sharp tongue, strangely enough, was one of the many reasons he'd adored her.

Jasper flopped back on the bed, lying on his side so he could gaze out through the sliding glass doors. The pool did look tempting, sparkles dancing on its aqua waters like diamonds. The whole view was like something stolen from a postcard, but taken circa 1965 or so.

Rob's house was not as big as Jasper had expected, but it was almost eerily midcentury modern, right down to the last detail. The furnishing, draperies, wood paneling, shag carpeting—they were all like something Rob had bought from various sets on the TV show *Mad Men*. Even the kitchen, all white and outfitted with turquoise appliances that Rob assured him were vintage inspired and not vintage, looked pulled from a time machine.

And the view outside? Good Lord. The pool was in the foreground, but beyond it rose a wall at least eight feet high. Fashioned from white brick, it was almost completely hidden under thick green foliage that made it appear the walls were fashioned from leaves. The wall surrounded the whole patio area, which was large and floored with stone. Lounge chairs, a seating area around a fire pit, and two dining tables, one round with a striped umbrella covering it and the other a long oblong glass-topped affair with seating for at least a dozen, made the pool area true outdoor living space. It was all done in bright white with orange accents.

Rob had pointed out a few of the plants strategically placed around the backyard. A couple of ocotillo trees rose, spire-like, near the pool's edge. There were barrel cacti and prickly pear. Torch lily and pencil cactus. All of them grew out of a rocky, boulder-strewn landscape in which Jasper would have assumed nothing could flourish.

And yet it did. Hummingbirds floated magically around the plants. Rob had told him to keep his eyes peeled for roadrunners, who were common but very quick to come and go.

As if all of this wasn't enough, beyond the walls the mountain range of San Jacinto rose up to an infinite sky.

"Fuck it," Jasper whispered to himself. "In for a penny, in for a pound." He didn't remember where he'd heard that phrase but thought it fit.

He wriggled out of his Levi's and shirt and stood for a moment near the screen door in nothing but his plaid boxers. Then he hooked his thumb in the waistband of those too.

Clothes simply seemed too confining for the desert.

As he stood naked by the glass doors, he took a deep breath, ready to take both a literal and metaphorical plunge.

"Go on," he heard Lacy urge in the back of his mind. "We only regret the things we didn't do..."

He eased open the slider and emerged into brilliant sunshine. He had next to no confidence, but that didn't have to show, now, did it?

With squared shoulders and chin up, he strode to the deep end of the pool as though he'd done it a thousand times. The truth was the only pool he'd ever swum in was the public one up the hill from his childhood home in Haddonfield.

He dove in and imagined himself parting the waters with a splash worthy of a David Hockney painting. Kicking, he swam the length of the pool underwater, then emerged, gasping for air, at the other end.

The first thing he saw when he broke the surface was a small white table. Rob had very stealthily left him a present—a clear plastic tumbler filled with crushed ice and liquid the color of cactus.

He pulled himself out and sat his ass on the hot stone next to the table. He took a sip. Tequila, jalapeno, cucumber, all danced across his tongue in one of the most flavorful libations he could honestly say he'd ever imbibed.

He looked around for Rob, wanting to express his appreciation for the drink, but he was nowhere in sight. All the oblong windows facing the pool were dark, throwing back reflections of sun and sparkling water.

Jasper shrugged, picked up his drink, and took another sip. He set it on a small white glass-topped table next to one of the orange-and-white mesh lounge chairs. He ducked back inside to grab a towel and spread it on the surface of the chair, where he reclined with his drink, reveling in the sun's heat and the slight breeze that blew down from the mountains.

He figured Rob would join him soon enough. In the meantime he wondered what a sunburned dick would feel like. He imagined it would hurt like hell.

When twenty sunny minutes or so had passed, Jasper wandered to the other side of the pool and found the bathroom Rob had mentioned earlier. It was large, with a walk-in shower paved in subway tile. Across from the shower were floor-to-ceiling shelves and arranged on them were an assortment of towels and bathing suits, not one of which was made for a female to wear.

Jasper wondered what kind of parties Rob had around this pool, how many naked men had dived into its waters.

Am I just another conquest?

He found a pair of Andrew Christian bright orange board shorts and slid into them. He wasn't brazen enough yet to wander around the house naked. Skinny-dipping was one thing...

Then he went into another pair of sliding doors that led into the kitchen. On the quartz-topped center island sat a glass pitcher of the margarita-like drink he'd enjoyed. Alongside the pitcher was a note:

> *Ran over to Jensen's to get supplies. Hope you're not a picky eater. Be back soon!*

Jasper figured Jensen's was a local grocery store and wondered what Rob would come back with. He refilled his glass and went back outside. This time he chose one of the seats around the big rectangular table.

He'd barely taken a sip when the doorbell rang. It sounded like Big Ben chimes, and Jasper laughed. Then he wondered who could be here. Had Rob forgotten his keys?

He got up from the table and made his way to the massive white double front doors. The doorbell sounded again before he could turn the doorknob.

When he opened it, a woman stood outside. She looked vaguely familiar, but Jasper couldn't immediately place her. She appeared to be about Rob's age, maybe a few years younger, and was almost painfully thin, dressed in a blousy satin top and palazzo pants, both in infused aquas and teals. She wore yellow espadrilles, and her hair was hidden under a big floppy straw hat. Most of her face, too, was concealed by a pair of dark Jackie O sunglasses.

"Who are you?" she asked. There was a grain of indignation in her tone.

Jasper assumed she was a neighbor but thought the query was a little rude. No hello or how do you do?

"I might ask you the same thing," Jasper said, softening the statement with a smile. Even though he wore a pair of swim trunks, he suddenly felt naked standing before her.

"I'm Eloise Burroughs, Rob's sister-in-law. And you are?"

It all clicked together. Jasper took an awkward step back, confused, a little shocked. Lacy's mom.

"Jasper. Jasper Warren. I was Lacy's, excuse me, Heather's, roommate in Chicago. I think we met briefly—" He cut himself off before he could say "at her wake."

"Of course." She nodded and then cocked her head to one side. "But what are you doing *here*?"

Jasper didn't know what to say, so he simply stood a little farther back. Besides, was what he was doing here really any of this woman's business? "You must be hot out there. Would you like to come in?"

She flounced by on a cloud of floral scent. Jasmine?

They stood in the dark foyer staring at each other for several moments. Jasper wanted to be the one to ask again what she was doing there but feared being so direct would be rude. He really had no place to ask.

So he put on his best smile. "Was Rob expecting you?"

"I don't see that that's any of your business. Is he home?"

"No. He went to the grocery store. Would you like to wait in the kitchen?" He pointed to it. "Or maybe out by the pool? Could I get you something to drink? There's a pitcher of some tasty cocktails in the kitchen."

She took off her sunglasses, it seemed, for the purpose of rolling her eyes. After a moment, she said, "I'll just wait in the living room. I don't need anything."

Jasper watched her step down into the sunken living room and take a seat on the big white sectional, which seemed to swallow her up.

"I'll just be in my room if you need anything." Jasper swallowed, suddenly feeling very nervous. He left her to hide.

In his room, Jasper thought, *Well, isn't this an odd turn of events? Odd enough that I'm here in Palm Springs, California, courtesy of a free, open-ended first-class ticket from perhaps the world's most famous author of psychological suspense; now I have to contend with being only one of a pair of visitors, both of whom loved a young woman whose life ended all too abruptly.* Jasper eyed his duffel, lying open on the floor, spilling the contents of his clothes as if it had exploded. *Or maybe the duct tape gave way?* he thought, causing his cheeks to burn once more with embarrassment.

He made his way over to dig through the clothes lying on the polished concrete floor. Even alone in his bedroom, he felt too raw in only a pair of shorts. He needed more to feel decent.

The jeans he'd worn earlier were near the top of the pile, and he yanked them on and pulled a black Obey T-shirt over his head.

He lay down across the bed. It had a white chenille bedspread that felt soft beneath him. But he couldn't relax, couldn't simply allow the time to pass until Rob returned, and perhaps he could get some answers to his questions.

Was it just a coincidence that Lacy's mother, of all people, turned up here on the very same day he arrived?

It wasn't out of the question, he concluded. She and Rob were, after all, family. Perhaps she came out west to visit him on a regular basis. Maybe their protocol was that there was no need to phone first. Open-door policy and all that.

Who knew?

Jasper sat up, nerves tingling like something small were scurrying beneath his skin. Once again, his mind went to the flee part of his fight-or-flee instinct, and he contemplated simply packing up his bag and calling an Uber to take him back to the airport. He could sit among the palm trees and wait for his flight home in the warm breeze. Even if it was a long wait, it wouldn't be so bad.

Before he had a chance to entertain this flight of fancy any further, he heard the front door open and close and Rob call out, "Jasper? You inside?"

Hand on the doorknob, Jasper paused when he heard Eloise say something. Her exact words weren't clear, but he imagined the look of surprise on Rob's face. That was, assuming he was surprised, but Jasper could imagine no earthly reason Rob would arrange for the two of them to be at his house at the very same time.

Jasper pressed his ear to the door and learned that he was right.

"Eloise? What on earth?" Rob asked. There was a small quiver to his voice, almost as though he were afraid.

"I needed to talk to you. Maybe we could have handled things over the phone or even email, but you're not responding to my calls or my texts. So I thought I'd take the bull by the horns as it were."

"Does my brother know you're here?"

"Of course. It was his idea. I was driving him nuts anyway. He probably just wanted to get rid of me, and now you feel the same, don't you? Well, it won't be so easy, my friend, as deleting a text."

"What are you talking about?"

"You have obligations to us, sir. Reparations to be made. And no, that is not high talk. I'll say it before you do. We've never dealt with what needed to be said. You've never done what needed to be done. I had hoped we could have a long talk at Heather's funeral, but you disappeared from the wake, and then I never saw you again. How could you just leave without saying goodbye to her? To us? You can't imagine our pain."

Her words had a certain timbre to them, Jasper imagined. *Almost as though she's on the verge of tears.*

"How could you just leave her like that?" Eloise paused, sniffled a little. "I guess it's par for the course."

Rob stammered, his words low and unintelligible. And then Jasper heard him say, "I couldn't stand it." And then, clearly, the sound of Rob crying.

Jasper cringed, wanting, out of decency, to pull away from the door, to stop this horrible eavesdropping, but he couldn't.

Rob said, "What might have been, Eloise. What might have been."

What the hell does that mean? Simply the promise of a life snuffed out too soon? Or is there more? Jasper slid to the floor, still keeping his head close to the crack between the door and its frame.

"Oh, Rob. She needed to know."

Now Jasper was even more confused. *Needed to know what?*

Rob's voice shifted from tearful to angry in a second. "You never had to tell her. And the way you told her! Shame on you! What purpose did it serve other than spinning her out of control? And look at how things ended up! Even if you really believed it was a good idea and not just some vindictive way to get back at me—and I think that's exactly the reason—the least you could have done was let me tell her. You couldn't even discuss it with me before you dropped that bomb on her!" No mistaking this last part—Rob shouted it. "You should have done the decent thing, the kind thing. Would that have been so hard?"

"She needed to know."

"Why? What difference would it have made? She didn't know for all these years."

"All these years, my dear, was much too long."

There was a long silence, so long that Jasper debated whether he should get up and join them. The tensions were so high, perhaps an interruption might be a saving grace.

"She was your *daughter,* Rob. She was your daughter. Was she *never* to know?"

Jasper shut his eyes and slumped even more.

He needed to get out of here.

Now.

Chapter Eight

Jasper didn't want to hear any more. He couldn't bear it. This was bizarro-world shit. This was out of the bounds of credulity or propriety. It was just *weird*.

Jasper wanted no part of it.

He put his earbuds in and plugged them into his phone. The Chainsmokers began singing "Selfie," and it immediately brought back memories of Lacy. They'd said the song was "their" song because they'd taken so many selfies of the pair of them—in the apartment, on Fargo beach, over at the Amber Waves Café, where they liked to go for breakfast when it was in the budget, out at the bars in Andersonville or along Halsted.

Jasper had a whole album of selfies of him and Lacy, some Snapchat enhanced, mostly just the pair of them.

He pressed his phone screen to advance to the next song. Beneath the music, he could hear Eloise and Rob arguing. Although he couldn't make out the words, he could decipher the emotions—the pain, the rage, the anguish.

This situation had been coming to a head for a long time. It was family drama. It had nothing to do with Jasper.

Except it did.

He'd loved Lacy. Like a sister. And his hurt was as real, if not even more authentic, than the two people arguing beyond his door.

I shouldn't be here. This is like some weird dream. I should actually be waking up in my own bed and scratching my head over what it all means.

He hurriedly stuffed his clothes into the duffel and then proceeded into the bathroom to swipe what few toiletries he'd brought into the bag too.

Finally, he stood near the sliding glass doors to call an Uber. The app quickly found him and told him a Toyota Prius driven by Brad would be arriving within twenty minutes.

He didn't want to walk by the combatants.

But there was no way out that he knew of other than going out of his bedroom and to the front door—crossing right by the bickering duo in the living room. He looked longingly at the sliders and the big wall beyond. Did it encircle the whole back? Surely there had to be a gate? Rob would have gardeners and pool boys coming in and out on a regular basis, right?

Jasper hoisted his duffel over his shoulder and headed out into what, just recently, had been a gorgeous spring day. Now there might as well have been thunderclouds, rain, and freezing wind—he felt so horrible, so sick.

So betrayed.

Why keep these secrets? From me? From each other?

Jasper thought his own tiny family unit was dysfunctional, but he and his dad appeared to have nothing on these people.

He skirted the pool and headed for the side of the house. Thank God, there was a mesh gate, bright white. He hurried to it.

It was locked with a keypad. Combination—so the gardener and pool boy could come and go.

Shit.

He went around the other side of the house and there was a gate there too.

Also locked.

Be a man.

He went back inside, took a deep breath, and then exited out his bedroom door, walking hurriedly, feeling as though it were *he* who had done something wrong. He kept his eyes on the prize, the front door, but his scalp tingled as he passed the living room. He was certain they were staring at him.

If his intuition hadn't informed him of this fact, then the sudden silence between them certainly provided a good clue.

But he didn't look. He didn't dare.

He opened the door and froze.

"Jasper?"

Rob.

Jasper wanted to run but could only stand there as he heard bare feet padding across the tile floor toward him. His spine stiffened.

As Rob neared him, Jasper was able to make himself turn.

When he saw the hurt on Rob's face, it just about killed him. *God, am I doing the right thing?* He could think of no words. His gut wrenched. His mouth went dry. He could hear the blood pounding in his ears.

"What's going on?" Rob glanced pointedly at the duffel bag—that tired, worn, and duct-taped symbol of his youth and poverty.

Jasper bit his lip and told himself to be a big boy. "I need to go home."

"Why?"

"This was a mistake."

Over Rob's shoulder, he could see Eloise emerge into the foyer. She stared at him, and he could read nothing in her bland, probably surgically enhanced, features.

"But you just got here."

Jasper nodded. "And I obviously had no idea what I was getting into."

"You don't understand."

"You're right about that. I don't have a fucking clue."

Before he could say any more, the sound of a car horn interrupted. It was his savior. Jasper glanced outside to the nearly empty street lined with palms and cacti. A black Prius idled across the desert-landscaped front yard. A figure in the driver's seat waved.

"I need to go. My ride's here."

Rob said, "You won't be able to get a flight just by walking up to a counter, you know. Stick around. We can make the arrangements together if you really want to leave."

"What's this kid doing here?" Eloise piped up. "Boy toy?"

Rob turned to look at her. "Will you please shut up?"

And that moment was all Jasper needed to hurry out the door and down the path to the street.

Even though Rob was calling him, and even though he was most likely right about Jasper not being able to get on a flight, he'd take his chances.

Without looking back, he opened the car door, flung his bag inside and himself after it. "The airport," he told the driver in a strangled voice.

"Which one, dude? Palm Springs? Ontario?"

Jasper couldn't understand the question, but he knew the right answer. "Palm Springs, of course." *Why would I want to go to Canada?*

"Sure." The driver put the car in gear and sped away.

Jasper could still hear Rob calling his name, even over the hum of the car's air conditioner. He closed his eyes, wishing he could do the same with his ears. He thought he'd hear Rob's plaintive cry long after he was out of earshot.

Chapter Nine

Jasper had nine hours to kill before getting on his flight back home to Chicago. Nine hours! He comforted himself that he was lucky he'd gotten anything at all in terms of an immediate flight even if his return was coach and involved two stops—Seattle, then back down to LA—before taking him home to O'Hare. The first layover would last six hours, the second one, two.

He wouldn't land in the Windy City until the next afternoon.

But at least he was going home—and relatively soon. The time was roughly equal to a shift at work, and this was, at least, way better. He wasn't folding clothes that he'd folded five minutes before. He wasn't trying to deal with returns of shoes that were three years old. He looked on the bright side—he could relax.

And about what had happened? The soap opera weirdness of it? He'd be okay. At least he'd extricated himself from what had to be one of the most potentially explosive and just plain odd circumstances he'd ever experienced in his young life.

Seriously, he couldn't imagine a more pleasant airport in which to wait out the majority of the time. He calmed himself sitting under a bright sky, warm sun, and palm trees. In the distance, he could see the majestic rise of the mountains. Every once in a while, a hummingbird would float by, its rapidly beating wings invisible. He had a latte from Starbucks and the latest Stephen King novel on his phone.

It could've been worse.

Later, he'd have a nice lunch at the outdoor café opposite and maybe treat himself to a couple of cosmopolitans, in honor of Lacy. He could do the same again for dinner. Then maybe he'd sleep or sleepwalk through all of this red-eye business.

What the hell had happened to Lacy, anyway?

Who was she?

He felt he knew who she was at her core—a sweet, kind, and loving young woman who'd been hurt somewhere along the way, so much so that she couldn't bear the chafing real life brings to us as an almost constant condition of use. She was afraid of people in general, and he was her shelter in the storm.

But what had made her that way? Underneath the goth trappings, she was beautiful, a voluptuous and earthy woman. Smart. Kind. Sensitive. At her best, Lacy had the power to charm and seduce anyone. Except she never wanted to. Staying home with Jasper, or acting as his wingperson, always seemed to be enough.

Until one tragic night, it wasn't.

Jasper would never understand. His own life was marred by serious tragedy, neglect, heartbreak, and pain. Most people's lives were, maybe not as severely as his own, but most people, like him, had one thing that kept them moving forward through life's darkest times—hope. They continued to know that nothing in this life, good, bad, or in between, was destined to last forever.

Everything changed.

He'd read somewhere once that everything in our lives was only given on loan, so what was the point in getting too attached or too wrapped up in, well, *anything*?

And now had come the news that Rob Burroughs, aka *New York Times* bestselling author Michael Blake, was not her uncle, which was surprising enough in itself because Lacy had never once deigned to mention the man, even when Jasper sat next to her on their couch reading one of his books, but her *father*. Her father? Who were the people claiming to be her parents, then? Was she adopted? Why the ruse?

This trail of thought was vicious and cyclical and only made Jasper's head hurt.

One of the great things about booze, Jasper thought as he stood up from his sun-warmed bench, *is that it has the power to bestow oblivion, right when I need it the most.*

He could taste the sweet yet potent blend of Cointreau, lime, vodka, and cranberry as he headed toward the airport's outdoor restaurant. Just thinking about that first sip did a lot to take his mind off his troubles, to ease the tension causing his shoulders to ride up.

As he neared the patio area of the restaurant, with its cheerful umbrella tables, he halted in his tracks, drawn rudely back to the present. Someone had shouted his name.

And who other than Mr. Robert Burroughs himself knew not only what he was called but that he would find him here?

Jasper turned slowly, the dread rising up once again in his gut.

There he was, a silhouette backlit by the sun and standing very still.

Jasper found no words coming to mind, let alone lips.

Rob moved closer, stepping into the same shadow Jasper himself occupied. Rob had changed into a pair of camouflage cargo shorts, a black T-shirt with the legend Desert Animal emblazoned across the chest, and a pair of flip-flops. The ensemble made him appear years younger, and Jasper wondered anew, for many reasons, why he'd found himself here in Southern California with this man. Younger looking or not, Rob would always be old enough to be his father. And Jasper was never the type to go after daddies, although there were many his age who did.

"What?" Jasper cocked his head. "What are you doing...?" his voice trailed off, and then he asked, "How did you get in here?" Pretty as it was, with its fresh breezes, arid desert air, sunshine, and palm trees all around, they were still in the boarding-gates area, only accessed by going through security with the proper ID and a boarding pass. People couldn't simply walk in. Those days were history, a time before Jasper could even recall.

"I came because I couldn't let you leave. Not in the way you did." Rob glanced back at the cheerful umbrella tables set out behind them, their sun-drenched optimism seeming out of sorts with the mood at hand. "Could I just talk to you, please?"

"I don't know" was the best Jasper could think to say.

Rob reached out as though to lay a hand on Jasper's shoulder. At the moment before he would have touched him, he seemed to think better of the notion and dropped his hand.

Jasper was relieved.

"Look. I know you must have lots of questions. Let me at least buy you something to drink? Maybe lunch? Would you be willing? Do you have time?"

Rob looked so hungry for some sign that Jasper would listen that Jasper, ever a softie, had to give in. "Okay. But first you have to tell me how you got beyond security. These days, that's not an easy task, if it's even a possible one."

Rob chuckled. "You're ignoring the obvious. But we'll get to that. Let's go grab a table before they all fill up."

He turned and started to head for the restaurant's entrance. Jasper wondered if Rob believed that if he didn't act quickly, he'd lose him.

Once they were seated, with a cosmo in front of Jasper and a scotch and a beer in front of Rob, they both grew quiet. Both studied the menu intently. Jasper wasn't hungry, not anymore. When their waiter returned for their order and Rob asked for a Cobb salad, Jasper said he'd have the same.

The waiter hurried away. He was slim, efficient, Hispanic, and had a great ass, which his tight black chinos showed off to good advantage. Jasper noticed because he was having difficulty meeting Rob's gray-blue eyes.

But finally he had to force himself to make eye contact. Rob was waiting like a good therapist.

"So are you gonna tell me?" Jasper took a sip of the cosmo. Pretty good but not as good as the ones he made.

"About Heather?"

"Yeah, I want to know all about that. But let's clear up the mystery of how you got by security and are sitting across from me."

"That bugs you, doesn't it?"

Jasper nodded. It did. But he could also acknowledge, at least to himself, that asking about this detail was an avoidance tactic. A warm breeze blew up, and Jasper could almost pretend this was a pleasant date. Almost.

Rob reached down to bring up something on his phone. He tapped and swiped and then showed Jasper the screen.

Boarding passes. For the same flights to Chicago that Jasper was on. There was something stalkerish about the move, and a small chill shivered through Jasper despite the sunshine and temperature.

After a moment, Jasper asked, "You fly coach?"

Rob laughed. "It was all they had. Sorry I couldn't get anywhere near you. I'm in the last row! In the middle. Do you know how long it's been since I've been so inconvenienced?"

"You're kidding, right?" Jasper could only think, *First world problems.*

"Maybe a little. Maybe not. I just haven't had to fly coach in a while."

"Must be nice." Jasper took another sip of his cocktail. He pointed to the phone's screen, and as he did, it faded to black. "So what's with the boarding pass? Just spend a few hundred so you could talk to me?" Jasper raised his eyebrows. "That must also be nice." He didn't really believe Rob was planning on flying later on tonight. To Chicago. With him.

Rob scratched his head and then gave him the sweetest, most sheepish smile Jasper had ever seen. "I was actually hoping to go with you. For a lot of reasons. The easiest one is I've never really spent any significant time in Chicago, and it seems like a great place. I've been in and out on book tours and once had the surreal but kind of wonderful experience of attending the International Mr. Leather competition one Memorial Day weekend many, many years ago when I was young and buff and looked good in a studded harness." He smiled and winked.

And Jasper bet he *still* looked good in a leather harness. Damn his false modesty.

"Anyway, I was hoping we could spend some time together on *your* home turf. Maybe, if you had time, you could show me the sights. I hear there's a wonderful architecture tour on the river. I'd like to see Millennium Park. Maybe hit the Art Institute and see its impressionist collection."

Jasper laughed at the absurdity of it all. "Wait. Let me get this straight—now you want me to play tour guide? You are one very strange man."

"Guilty. And yes, I do." Rob reached across the table and covered Jasper's hand with his own. He squeezed gently and then left the touch there—electric. "Look. I know you're confused. I know this is a hell of a lot. If I wrote down what you've seen lately, the conversation you've overheard, I think my agent would send it back to me. She'd say, 'Rob, I can't sell this. Nobody'd believe it. They'd think you're off your rocker. Now *I* know that's true, but your readers don't have to.'" He chuckled and his gaze went faraway for a moment as Jasper presumed he imagined his agent.

Jasper imagined her too—as Lauren Bacall in some Fifth Avenue high-rise office building. "Truth is stranger than fiction, right?"

"Definitely in this case. And I want you to know everything.

"But I also want to get to know you better. That day after Heather's wake, I felt a connection. And I don't often feel that. And then when we started emailing each other, I came to know a guy far beyond his years in wisdom and maturity. If I hadn't met you in person and known your age, I would have guessed you were much older—and I mean that as a compliment. I've never been the kind of gay man who chases after boys, hoping they're into daddies. That scene is fine for some, but it's never been for me. I've dedicated so much of my life to career that I haven't had much in the way of romance, but what attempts I've made have always been with men my own age, or even older. I know, I know—don't even bother to wonder if *they're* still alive."

They both laughed at that. And Jasper could sense, a little, the tension beginning to ease between them. Their waiter brought their salads and asked if they'd like more drinks. Rob said, "We must have another round. Our flight is eight hours away." And suddenly, the idea of *that* seemed very funny as well.

Rob went on, "I know I scared you away. So let's take this horrible flight together. I'll get a room downtown somewhere, and we can hang out. No pressure."

"And you'll tell me the story? All about Heather?"

Rob nodded and tears sprang to his eyes.

"Yes. Yes. And you'll tell me your story too. 'Cause I live for stories."

Jasper began eating. He didn't know whose story would be more incredible.

He'd switched his phone off, but he noticed the screen come to life as the phone vibrated. Dad was calling.

"Do you need to get that?" Rob asked.

"Not now." Jasper sent the call to voicemail.

Chapter Ten

They landed at O'Hare tired and grouchy. Rob hadn't been able to sleep a wink, and when he caught up to Jasper in the terminal (Jasper had *not* waited for him), he figured the same was true for him. Rob didn't want to make things worse by saying out loud the teasing joke that came to mind: "Now you *do* look close to my age."

But it was true. Jasper had bags under his eyes. His hair was mussed, and his clothes, if not his face, were wrinkled.

"Hey, hey, Jasper! Wait up!" Rob tried hard to keep his tone of annoyance at bay.

Jasper whirled on him. When Rob saw the look on his face, he questioned if he'd made a mistake. He figured Jasper's features, lips drawn into a thin line and eyes narrowed, only softened because it sunk in for Jasper how stunned and hurt Rob was at his expression. "I'm sorry," Rob muttered. "But I just wondered—"

Jasper cut him off. "I'm so fucking tired. I don't mean to be a dick. But, uh, what's your plan?"

"My plan?"

"Yeah. I mean, like, where are you gonna stay?" Jasper glanced down at the floor for a minute and then back up at Rob. "I've got a roommate, and we're crowded into a little one-bedroom on the Far North Side. It's about the size of your master bathroom." He grinned, and for a moment and despite what he was saying, his face lit up with a kind of radiance. "I couldn't let you stay with me if I wanted to."

Rob really hadn't counted on Jasper putting him up. And he bristled at him saying *if he wanted to* as though the implication was, he didn't. *Good God*, Rob wondered, *have I become a joke? An old man chasing after a young one, a la* Death in Venice?

Of course, it had been a long and certainly impulse-driven trip. Rob had never been prone to such literal flights of fancy. But there was something about this young man that touched him deeper than mere lust. It was as though Jasper had grasped and held on to not only his heart, but also his soul. Rob felt compelled to explore this attraction further.

But Jasper was right in wondering what was going on—what his *plan* was. After what they'd just been through, Rob knew staying with Jasper would be completely out of the question. Besides, he was aware of Jasper's moderate circumstances and understood things like guest rooms were luxuries he couldn't afford. And sleeping next to him? While that might be wonderful to imagine, they were a long way from that point. Especially now.

So he'd made arrangements at the airport before they'd left. "As I mentioned, I'll stay at a hotel downtown." He didn't want to mention the Four Seasons, because it seemed boastful, but that was where he'd be.

Jasper smiled again, and Rob melted a little more. Here was a young man whose smile certainly fit the old cliché about lighting up a room. And what was better was that he had no idea how beautiful he was. Men were always more attractive, Rob thought, when they were unaware of the spell they cast.

Jasper put a hand on his arm. He looked contrite. "Listen, we're both worn out. I'm gonna go home and take advantage of the one thing that's truly, truly magical about the old run-down apartment I live in—its original claw-foot tub—and take a long bath. And don't tease me about being girly—I will use bubble bath and lots of candles. I will play some Adele through my Bluetooth speaker. And then I'm going to crawl into bed, not with you, but with Stephen King, and try to read for maybe five minutes before I drop off and sleep for hours and hours.

"And then, when morning comes and I've had my coffee, I will call you. We will make plans to do some sightseeing, but most of all, to talk. I need to hear how the real Michael Blake tells a story—especially a true one with a main character I loved a lot.

"Does that sound okay?"

Actually, it did sound okay. Better than. Rob was worn thin too. His eyes burned. His limbs felt weighed down, as though gravity pulled harder now that they were on the ground again. He knew who the "main character" Jasper loved a lot was. Rob stared at Jasper for a moment with a lump in his throat, tears welling up in his eyes, but he held back.

His own daughter, Heather, had been cast in that role thirty some years ago, when Rob was still trying to figure out who—and what—he was. Rob didn't understand why, but he would let Jasper know everything about their relationship, their wonderful closeness, the cocoon they'd built around themselves, the way their minds melded, the way they could make each other laugh, the tight, loving bond unlike any other...

Until it had all been destroyed. And Rob knew that was his fault. And yet, he felt compelled to lay it all before this young man. His greatest shame. His heartbreak.

And he prayed that, if Jasper could not forgive him, he could at least understand.

Jasper snapped him out of his reverie, which had morphed into an image of Heather, beautiful brunette Heather, laughing at something Rob said as they sat together in his hot tub one winter night underneath a blanket of desert stars.

"Dude. I'm beat. I gotta go. Did you hear me?"

Rob smiled sadly and nodded. "You'll call me in the morning."

Jasper gave him a quick nod. "I need to go."

"You *will* call?"

"Don't underestimate yourself. I got your number."

And with those words, Jasper vanished into the crush of hurrying travelers.

Rob watched him until he disappeared. It took everything he had not to run after him. But he reminded himself of *Death in Venice. Have some dignity, man, for God's sake, have a little dignity.*

As he waited for a break in the crowd, he remembered a line from *Death in Venice*: "Like any lover, he desired to please; suffered agonies at the thought of failure." He moved toward the Ground Transportation sign, thinking the quote was apt.

Chapter Eleven

Jasper slept deeply. He'd awakened around 4:00 a.m. to an L train making sparks and cackling as it rushed by his window, impatient to make its standing date at the end of the red line, Howard Street. He'd gotten up then to pee and returned to bed to fall back into the kind of sleep that's so deep, it's a near coma, experienced only in the very early morning.

And he dreamed.

He held his mother's hand, and as he did so, he peered up at her—her honey-colored hair, cut in a bob that ended at her shoulders, her wide hazel eyes glancing down at him with love. Her scoop-necked turquoise sundress was pushed out by her bulging belly. A charm bracelet rattled on her tan wrist.

Ahead of them, a stroller containing his baby sister rolled through a crowded and dirty used-furniture store. His baby sister cooed, clutching a red-and-blue rattle in her pudgy fist.

The concrete floor beneath their feet was gritty, worn, cracked.

And then the realization came, even in the dream, where they were. With that knowledge, everything changed. The sun outside, so bright just a second ago, the very essence of summer, vanished behind a cloud. The store went eerily silent as the fluorescent lighting flickered and then darkened, its buzz coming to an abrupt halt.

With the store plunged into darkness, the only light source was the muted sun outside. It was the calm before a very bad storm.

Jasper clung tighter to his mother's hand. "Mama, what's happening?"

"Shhh. Don't worry." She stopped pushing the stroller long enough to kneel down beside him. She touched his cheek and said in a very soft voice, "It will happen so fast, we won't feel a thing. No pain. Just a moment of surprise and then it'll be over, no worse than getting a shot." She handed him a Tootsie Roll, folding his fingers around the candy. "You weren't even here."

She let go of his hand and stood. He wanted to run after her, but she moved forward into the shadows. He stood rooted to the spot, frozen by terror and expectation.

Two figures, black, crafted from shadows, separated themselves from the darkness and moved toward his mother, impossibly quick. A pair of upholstery shears glinted in the gloom, contrary to reality.

A sharp intake of breath, just before a scream.

A song began playing. The same few notes over and over. Urgent.

Jasper opened his eyes to his phone, playing its ringtone and vibrating on the nightstand next to his bed. On a lark, without really knowing why, he'd assigned the Jack Sparrow theme song to his father once upon a time.

He groaned and rubbed his eyes. Sat up and yawned.

The dream and its horrific images departed. And Jasper had no desire to cling to them. He mumbled, unsure even why, "I wasn't there anyway."

He couldn't avoid his dad forever. And it wasn't like him to call so many times in just a few days. Hell, it wasn't like him to call at all, save for Jasper's birthday and on Christmas.

He poked at the screen. "Dad." Jasper's voice came out in a rasp.

"Were you sleeping?"

Jasper glanced down at the phone's screen. "Well yeah, it's only a little after five here."

"Shit. I'm sorry, son. But I've been hopin' I could get ahold of you. Didn't you see I been trying to call?"

Leave it to his dad to rely on caller ID, rather than stoop to leaving a message. His dad had always been the most taciturn man Jasper had ever known. It was as though talking actually caused him physical pain. And maybe it did.

It was probably torture for him to leave a recorded message.

Nevertheless, "Yeah, I saw. I went out of town." Jasper knew his father wouldn't ask where he'd been.

And he was right. "I was trying to call you because I didn't know if you'd heard about Louise."

Jasper sat up straighter in his bed, suddenly more awake and alert. "Louise? What about her?"

Louise Bell had lived next door to Jasper and his father since before his mom and little sister had been murdered, that horrible summer day all those years ago. Jasper had a brief flash of his dream and quickly banished it to whatever oblivion dreams lived in.

She'd been a kind of surrogate mother to Jasper, babysitting him when his father worked and Jasper wasn't in school. Jasper could count on her to be there when he came home from Pulaski Elementary, seated in her warm maple-and-gold kitchen at the table, working a crossword puzzle. The kitchen was always redolent with the smell of baked goods—fresh bread, sweet-potato pie, glazed doughnuts. There was always something sweet for him.

And for her. Louise probably weighed a good three hundred pounds, but her bosom, underneath the simple floral-print housedresses she favored, was always soft, smelling of baby powder. Her freckles, dark skin, and short afro rose up in Jasper's memory, the backdrop to her smile, which was always loving, save for the times when he dared to bother her when she was watching what she called her stories, *All My Children* and *The Bold and the Beautiful*. Those times, Jasper was expected to maintain his silence.

Louise and her large extended clan—her husband, Jessie, and her three grown kids and countless grandkids—had taken Jasper and his reluctant father into their family. Without Louise and her endlessly kind heart, Jasper would have been alone on many holidays, watching TV with his dad while it seemed the whole world, except for them, celebrated.

"Well, I don't know quite how to tell you this, son—"

Jasper felt a lurch in his gut, in his heart. *Please no. Hasn't there been enough pain?* "She's okay, right?"

Jasper knew Louise had a heart condition, high blood pressure, and diabetes. She also had an infinite capacity for cooking and taking care of her loved ones. Relaxation wasn't in her vocabulary.

His father didn't answer directly. "She hosted one of her legendary Sunday dinners." Three kinds of meat—poultry, ham, and beef—macaroni and cheese, black-eyed peas, collards, corn bread, pies, cakes, and biscuits were typical fare, and Louise wouldn't hear of letting anyone else make anything. "Nobody does it better," she'd whisper to little Jasper when he'd ask why. She'd laugh and tap her chest. "Baby, nobody else's tastes as good as mine. And that's not bragging. That's the simple truth."

"And?" Jasper knew what was coming, could almost feel it like a wrecking ball headed in his direction. He closed his eyes and his shoulders rose up, almost as though he were expecting a physical blow.

The news was worse. "She collapsed in the kitchen. I watched it all from the backyard. The ambulance showed up. EMTs tried their best."

"So they tried their best?" *Please say something other than what I know I'm going to hear. Say,* "And they brought her back. But, man, was it ever a close call!"

But that's not what Dad said.

Jasper heard his own voice break as he said, "Please, Dad, don't say it. Please."

There was silence on the other end for too long. "Spare me," Jasper wanted to add. "As long as you don't say the words, it can't be true."

"Aw, son, I wish I didn't have to tell you this. I'm sorry, Jazz, but she's gone."

Jasper was tempted to simply end the call. Dad would probably be grateful. It was hard enough for him to make simple everyday conversation, let alone one like this.

When his father spoke again, Jasper was surprised. "She loved you just as much as any of her own. Hell, you *were* one of her own—sometimes it's about more than blood to make a family. You know that, huh?"

Jasper was weeping, but wanted, who knew why, to withhold that fact from his dad. "Yeah, yeah." He sniffed and drew in a deep breath. "Was it at least fast? Was there just a moment of surprise, and then it was all over?" It wouldn't occur to Jasper until much later that he'd repeated the dream words of his mother at that moment.

"I think it was. She was making one of her famous feasts. Everybody was there. It was a party. I like to think Louise is looking down now, glad she went the way she did, with people she loved, cooking for them. How could it possibly be any better?"

"That was her joy," Jasper said. He refrained from commenting that the words his dad spoke were the most he'd heard him speak all at once in many years. It warmed Jasper's heart to know Dad was trying, in his simple way, to comfort him.

Jasper blurted, "How are you? Doing okay?"

His father, again, was quiet for a long time. Jasper wondered if he was only imagining the sound of his father softly crying. "You know I'm sad. She was a big part of life. She was *bigger* than life." He chuckled. "In more ways than one."

Jasper chuckled back. "That's for sure." He paused again. "When's the funeral?"

His father drew in a deep breath. "That's why I've been calling. I wanted to see if you could get back here in time. But son, I'm sorry, she's already been laid to rest up at the cemetery on the hill."

"Pleasant View?"

"That's the one."

Jasper felt a moment of rage—that he didn't know, that he'd missed a chance to say goodbye, to see her, maybe, one last time. He would bet she'd clung to a Bible and a cross in her casket. The rage vanished quickly once he realized he had no one to direct it toward, save himself.

Jasper realized they'd run out of things to talk about. This was the way it always was. Information imparted. Absorbed. And then it was time to move on.

"Okay, Dad. Everything else okay?"

"Sure. Same old, same old. They're putting in a Walmart out by the highway."

"How about that?" Jasper said, and then his mind went blank, so he simply added, "You take care."

"You too."

Jasper was about to hang up when his dad said, "Jasper?"

"Yeah?"

His dad paused again, as though to gather up the courage to say what was coming. "I love you, son," he said in a rush.

And Jasper was stunned. He'd never heard these words before. He was sure of it. He almost hung up. But just as rushed, he said the words back. "Love you too."

Then he hung up, very quickly.

He was trembling.

*

Jasper spent a long time in the shower after the call. He simply let the hot water cascade over him as he tried to absorb the loss of the woman who was, for all intents and purposes, his second mother. How did he manage to have such lousy luck as to lose not one, but two moms in the course of his young life? He could believe the universe had decided he had no need for a mother at all.

He recalled Louise, who, it seemed, always sat in her gold, brown, and maple kitchen. Even when she watched TV, she never went into the living room where the big color set was, but instead would station herself at the round kitchen table and watch her stories on a little portable on a hutch across from her.

He imagined himself leaning over her on the floor of that kitchen, leaning close to her freckled face with its broad nose and full lips, and kissing her one last time before she expired. Telling her he loved her with all of his heart.

He liked to believe she knew, even now.

He didn't know, really, how to come to terms with her passing. He had a feeling that time wouldn't come until he returned to southern Illinois someday, when he could visit her grave. He'd put flowers—lilies, her favorite—on it and talk to her for a while, letting her know all the ways she'd made a difference in his life and how much he loved her.

And then came the thought of his dad telling him he loved him. That was amazing, a true first, but Jasper still felt numb. In shock, he supposed, over Louise's passing and the fact that he'd actually uttered words Jasper had longed to hear all his life.

When he was done, he took his time drying off. Standing in the living room in a pair of worn flannel boxers, he noticed how bright the sunlight was that day—as though spring had finally arrived and was announcing its presence with gilded illumination. The rays coming in through the big windows were golden shafts, piercing through any kind of darkness hanging heavy in the apartment.

He sat down on the couch and wondered if he should call Rob or not. There was a big part of him that wanted to comfort himself by crawling back into bed, turning on the TV, and bingeing on the old movies he adored. Maybe something directed by Douglas Sirk or Howard Hawks or Frank Capra. He'd finish up the Ben and Jerry's in the freezer. He'd sleep. Wake up and repeat the whole self-indulgent process.

He had to admit, the notion had its appeal.

But Rob had come all this way. And he was waiting for Jasper's call at some hotel in downtown Chicago, most likely somewhere along the rarified part of North Michigan Avenue referred to as the Magnificent Mile. Jasper pictured him standing with room service coffee at floor-to-ceiling windows, a fluffy white robe covering him as he looked out at the shimmering blue-green expanse of Lake Michigan.

It wasn't only that Jasper felt obligated to call, even if he did. The main thing was that he really wanted to see Rob. They'd yet to connect as he somehow knew they could, and he ached for that to happen, especially now, sitting here with the residue of pain clinging so heavily to his heart.

So he picked up his phone.

Rob answered on the first ring. "You called."

"I said I would."

"I know you did, but what we have here is a bit of an odd situation in many ways. I was just sitting here with my Earl Grey trying to convince myself that you weren't going to call and that I should just accept it and move on."

"That's defeatist."

"It's realistic." Jasper heard him take a sip, noting that he'd been wrong about the coffee. He was still imagining the fluffy white robe, though. It hung loosely open, revealing a lean and tanned body dusted with dark hair.

"Well, we're just talkin' here, supposin'," Jasper said. "I'm still off. It's a gorgeous day out there, and you told me you didn't know Chicago very well."

"I'm lookin' for a guide. A cute one."

"At your service, sir."

"I can send a car up to you."

Jasper let that sink in. He shook his head. The idea was too *Pretty Woman* for him. "Or I could just hop on the L and come to you. I just had my shower, so all I need to do is throw on some clothes and be on my way. Depending on exactly where you are, I could be to you, with any luck, within the hour."

"That would be lucky, wouldn't it?"

"You bet it would." Jasper smiled and felt a little unburdened. "So? Are you gonna tell me where you are, or do I have to wander around the Near North Side, asking hotel concierges if you're staying with them?"

"You're a smartass."

"And proud of it. Come on, don't be shy. The Heart O' Chicago?" Jasper laughed at imagining Rob staying at what could only be called a discount motel near the far-north thoroughfares of Clark and Ridge.

"I don't know that one, but I have a feeling you're making fun of me." Rob paused. "I'm at the Four Seasons, downtown."

"Figures. Although you're not technically downtown. You're too far north for that." Jasper wasn't in the mood for a geography lesson and figured Rob really wouldn't care. Feeling like a trick on Grindr, he said, "I'm on my way."

"Okay, cool. See you soon."

Jasper hung up. And it was on.

*

On Delaware Place, Jasper paused outside the entrance to the Four Seasons. He'd actually been inside the luxury hotel once before, but he didn't think he'd share that experience with Rob.

It had been one of the sleazier moments in his adult life, a hookup with three other guys who'd all, one after the other, had their way with him.

The odd thing he remembered most vividly about that encounter was how the host—a guy named Miles— had ordered room service for him after the other two left. They'd eaten cold poached salmon with sour cream and dill, roasted fingerling potatoes, and an arugula salad with a lemon vinaigrette.

Jasper couldn't remember even one of their faces, let alone any other parts of their anatomy, although he supposed he *did* have a good time. Didn't he?

The salmon had been delicious.

He shrugged and moved toward the doorman stationed outside the Four Seasons' revolving doors.

Inside, he moved quickly through the lobby and headed for the bank of elevators, hoping this second experience within the walls of the deluxe hotel would prove more memorable.

Maybe he'd changed.

He stood outside Rob's door for the longest time, debating. He could always turn and go back home. It wasn't too late. He could explain that he'd lost a woman who'd been like a mom to him and that he needed to grieve, which was true enough.

But Louise wouldn't have approved of him using her as an excuse not to move forward with his life, no matter how much the loss of her affected him. He remembered that winter day when he was a senior in high school and had come out to her, in that very same kitchen where so many memories gathered and lived. He'd been so scared he'd been shaking as he sat at the table, toying with a piece of sweet-potato pie and a cup of coffee.

He worried Louise wouldn't love him anymore. After all, she was old school, raised on the South Side of Chicago in the Baptist faith. Jesus was a personal friend. She wore a hat to church on Sunday and sang gospel hymns in the choir.

After he'd managed to choke out the words, "I'm gay," she looked at him with those warm brown eyes of hers. And then she threw back her head and laughed.

"What's so funny?"

"You think I didn't know that?"

"You did?" Jasper could distinctly recall his shock as a physical sensation—a single drop of sweat rolling down his spine.

"Of course I did. Me and everyone else who's ever come into contact with you." She wiped a tear from the corner of her eye. "You thought it was some big secret?"

Jasper had finally laughed—a little—himself. "I guess." He made himself take a sip of coffee. "And you don't think any less of me? Don't think I'm gonna burn in Hell?"

"Sweetie, you might burn in Hell, but not for being gay." She touched his cheek with her careworn hand. "You're one of God's own children. He's not gonna fault you for being who you are. And neither am I."

Jasper moved closer to Rob's door. One thing she'd said stood out. "The only thing I could be mad at you for, honey, is not finding love. Because in the end, that's our greatest gift. It's our power, our blessing, and our reason for living."

Louise wouldn't want him to turn away from this door.

So he raised his hand and knocked, for Louise, for himself.

Rob opened the door almost before Jasper could lower his hand back to his side.

The sunlight from the windows behind him made him a silhouette. Almost.

Jasper felt like he was seeing him for the very first time. Not just how handsome he was—he was that, in spades—but a vulnerability there, a hope written in the way he bit his lower lip, a calmness, yet an excitement too.

"I'm so glad you're here."

The words could have been a cliché, cheap sentiment, something one says like "Pleased to meet you," but Jasper felt like Rob meant the simple statement with his heart, meant it deep down.

It was a charged moment. Something like electricity—perhaps he could call it anticipation—hung in the air as they stood facing each other, one outside and one in.

Stepping across that threshold would change Jasper's life. It wasn't a conscious notion, but something he felt deep inside, instinctively. He wanted to rush into Rob's arms, but propriety—and nothing more than that, really—held him back.

Louise, if she'd been there, would have pushed him, laughing.

Finally, Rob stepped back and at the same time opened the door wider. "Come on in."

Their day together was about to begin.

Jasper took in the mussed king-size bed, the view of downtown buildings, the sunlight glinting off their glass facades, in a single glance.

He didn't want this to be a tawdry encounter, one where he offered himself up like some sacrificial lamb, but maybe, just maybe, the beginning of something real.

"I wish every day could be like this." Jasper went to gaze out the window at the majesty of the day and the buildings men had built almost as though to worship the sunlight and the cloud-choked, yet sun-drenched, sky.

Chapter Twelve

"I wish every day could be like this."

Rob considered the back of Jasper's head as he stared out the window at the perfection of the spring day—his dark, wavy hair, the alert way his head sat upon those beautiful and broad shoulders. Rob needed to say something but wasn't quite sure what, so he asked, "How shall we make the best of it?"

Jasper turned to him, and Rob noticed, not for the first time, how clear and magnetic the green of his eyes was. He savored the sharp planes of Jasper's face, softened by the dark stubble on his cheeks and chin. Complementing those features were his full lips and strong, aquiline nose.

"Do you have a car?" Jasper asked.

"No, but I'm sure we could rent one."

"There's lots to see downtown. I mean, we could just head out the front door, see Water Tower Place and then stroll down Michigan Avenue, see sights like the Tribune Tower, the Wrigley Building, stuff like that. We'd avert our eyes as we passed the Trump Tower, of course." Jasper laughed and eyed Rob with a little questioning look in his eyes.

"What?" Rob asked. "Are you wondering if I'm a Republican?"

Jasper cocked his head and narrowed his eyes. "If you are, I'll just be on my way. It's what I call cutting my losses."

"What do you think? I'm not one of those Log Cabin nutjobs, for heaven's sakes. No, if I leaned any further left, I'd fall over." Rob swallowed back another laugh. "So what are you thinking?"

"As I was saying, we *could* just walk down Michigan Avenue. Lots to see. Lots of restaurants and stores you'd only find on Rodeo Drive in Beverly Hills. At least I think so."

"You didn't stay in California long enough to—"

Jasper cut him off before, Rob supposed, he could say anything embarrassing or chiding. "And, of course, there's Millennium Park and the Bean and so on and so forth. Navy Pier. The Ferris wheel."

"All the touristy stuff," Rob said.

"Yeah. And there's nothing wrong with that. They can all be fun and interesting." Jasper moved away from the window and sat down on the love seat nearby. He seemed to be relaxing a bit. "But, if we had a car, I'm thinking I could show you some of my favorite places. You know, the kind of stuff that's off the beaten path. We can do the touristy stuff maybe later, time permitting."

Rob came and sat down beside Jasper, close enough that their bodies barely touched, but that touch was electric, like something charged against his skin, sparking. "Now you're speaking my language. I want to see the Chicago you know, the one that tourists don't see."

Jasper laid his head on Rob's shoulder for a moment. "Then let's do it. I have a few places in mind."

Rob didn't want to move, didn't want to disturb that comfortable weight of Jasper's head on his shoulder. It felt *right*. But Jasper ended the sensation for him, so Rob stood. "I'll call downstairs, see if maybe the concierge can set up a car for that." He headed for the phone on the desk

"Wait. Forget the car. Let's travel like the people do." Jasper grinned when Rob turned to look at him.

*

The subway car was crowded. Rob felt like an old man, truly this time, because Jasper had insisted he take the only available seat in the car when they boarded at Chicago Avenue. But hell, Rob was old enough to be Jasper's dad, so why kid himself? Besides, it put his eyes level with Jasper's crotch, and that was no *small* consolation. After stopping at Clark and Division, the train car was truly in line with the old expression "packed in like sardines."

Jasper leaned down to whisper, "It's not usually this crowded so late in the morning. Must have been a long gap between trains."

Rob wondered if his white privilege and wealth were showing. Was he wrinkling his nose at the smells, which seemed to be predominantly sweat, motor oil, and fried chicken? Was he leaning away too obviously from the hipster next to him—dressed in Nirvana flannels, ripped jeans, and nodding off every few minutes to lay his head on Rob's shoulder? Was he too wide-eyed at the assortment of people on the train? There was everything from Loyola and Northwestern college students to business types in suits to one guy in running shorts and nothing else, to a bicyclist all in spandex, to a couple of pregnant women. Nearly every age and ethnicity were represented.

Rob realized how sheltered he'd been most of his life. He'd grown up privileged on Long Island, the son of a highly successful hedge-fund manager, and becoming rich and famous in his own right had always seemed like his due, nothing special in his neck of the woods.

He didn't want to admit to Jasper that this train ride was his first on public transportation. Why, even during his many trips to Manhattan to meet with agents, publicists, and editors, he always traveled by private car with a driver, which was why he couldn't help but wonder if he stood out now as someone who didn't quite fit in.

What are you thinking? That's elitist! The truth is you don't look any different from anyone else. Some of these folks are dressed worse than you and some better. Rob looked down at his jeans and Grace Jones caricature black T-shirt, his black Cons. He had Jasper to thank for the fashion sense. He'd had on an Izod and pressed khakis before Jasper had eyed him up and down, saying, "Dude. Seriously?"

It was impossible to talk to Jasper, and that was kind of a relief because Rob fell into writer mode, wanting to take it all in. The crush of people. The diversity. And once they passed out of the North and Clybourn station, they rose up into the light as they emerged from the subway to stop at Fullerton Avenue.

The difference seemed as metaphorical as it was real.

The sunlight cleansed the car somehow, making its interior less close, less crowded. It also helped that now they were north of the downtown, fewer people were getting on than were getting off.

Finally, Jasper could sit down beside him. He leaned into Rob a little, nudging him with his shoulder.

"How many stops to your place?" Rob asked.

Jasper eyed him. "Stop it. We're not going there. A dozen or so. I don't count them." He grinned, and Rob could see the little boy beneath the stubble and the killer model looks. "Well, actually, I do. I ride these damn trains so much I *do* know. It's a dozen, an even dozen. Next is

Addison, then Sheridan, then Wilson, then Lawrence, Argyle, Berwyn, Bryn Mawr, Thorndale, Granville, Loyola, Morse, and then Jarvis, my stop. Rogers Park.

"We'll be getting off at Bryn Mawr." Jasper raised his eyebrows. "And then it's a good thing it's a nice day because we'll have a bit of a hike ahead of us." He paused. "Unless you wanna grab a cab, which I'm sure we can."

Rob laughed. "What? You think I'm too old and feeble to handle a city walk?" He shook his head. "Jesus. I'll have you know that this guy—" He tapped his chest with his thumb. "—this guy has hiked several of the more challenging trails at Joshua Tree and lived to tell about it. I've done the Spitler Peak trail in the San Jacintos. Just to name a few. Next time you come out to Palm Springs, we'll get you out on one of the desert hiking trails and see how you do."

"No need to take offense. I was just asking." Jasper stood as the train pulled into Bryn Mawr station.

They emerged onto a bustling city street. Looking toward the east, Rob could see the broad blue expanse of Lake Michigan nearby—only a few blocks. White sparkles danced on the water's surface, and he was so tempted to say, "Let's just head to the beach," but this was Jasper's day, Jasper's show, and Rob knew he should let him run things.

They turned away from the lakefront and began heading west.

"Where are we going, anyway?"

"You'll see."

*

"You brought me to a cemetery?" Rob stood beside Jasper across from the front gates of Rosehill Cemetery, peering up at the limestone front gate. It was a massive castellated Gothic structure, and Rob could almost envision a castle rising up beyond this entrance. Hell, the gate itself looked as though it should *be* part of a castle.

"I brought you to one of my favorite places in Chicago that just happens to be a cemetery," Jasper explained. "It's beautiful in there. Lots of famous people buried there, lots of gorgeous memorials and crypts. Swans. Ponds. Green grass and trees. And it's all right in the middle of the northwest side of the city. You head through those gates and there's peace. Quiet. Serenity. If you allow it." Jasper smiled. Rob could see the innocent pleasure Jasper took from being here.

And Rob didn't want to spoil that naïve bliss commenting on how odd it was to take him to a cemetery as the first stop on his sightseeing tour of Chicago, especially in light of the fact that it was the recent death of someone they both loved that had brought them together.

So he kept those thoughts to himself.

"I'll give you a little walking tour." Jasper led him toward the Gothic portal. He pointed out a set of old stone stairs, covered in vines. Rob wondered if it was a kind of monument in itself, perhaps trying to make a statement about the relentless encroachment of life even in the face of death.

"Those steps used to lead up to a train station on the Chicago Northwestern line. It was where funeral cars on the train could be met. At least that's what I always heard. Hasn't been used, obviously, for that purpose in years."

"Wow," Rob marveled.

They stepped inside the cemetery proper, and Rob wondered if the change he noted was only in his imagination. But it did seem cooler suddenly, the sounds of traffic and trains diminishing.

The sun beat down on them, but Rob felt cold anyway. This couldn't be the same sun that shined so brutally on him in the desert, could it? "This must be a different sun, a cooler one," he told Jasper, who said nothing and only eyed him with a little amused suspicion.

They'd walked a long way to get here and now, Jasper told him, they were going to walk a lot more. They passed mausoleums with ornate architecture and stained glass. A monument to soldiers and sailors. The graves of Union soldiers and generals alike.

They stopped at one breathtaking grave, and Jasper put his palm lightly on the large glass case that held the reclining figure of a young woman with a child in her arms.

"Oh my God," Robert said. "That's amazing."

"It's a mother who died in childbirth and her daughter. The dad, Horatio Stone, commissioned the sculpture." Jasper gazed into Rob's eyes. "They say it's haunted, and that around Halloween, the glass case fills with a white mist."

"Really?" Rob felt a chill run up his spine.

"We were never able to confirm it."

"We?" Rob asked.

"Lacy and me. Or Heather, as you called her." Jasper started walking away from the tragically beautiful mother-and-child monument. He didn't look at Rob as he explained, "This was one of our favorite places to come on days off. It didn't matter what the weather was like. Sunny, like this, Rosehill is a place of tranquility. But on cold, gray, and drizzly days, it was something else entirely. Not spooky, like you might think, but just...sad. 'Melancholy' is what Lacy called it."

They walked in silence for a while, passing more monuments and graves, elaborate and simple, all in tribute to souls now gone. Some memorials were so old the names had worn off, and Rob supposed anyone who knew who the tribute was for had long ago passed away too.

How long does it take before no one remembers us? How long does it take until there's no one left on earth whom we've touched?

They came upon a beautiful pond that looked like something out of a picture book (as long as you didn't mind the goose crap all around its edges), with mesmerizing, sunlit emerald water upon which a lone swan and a couple of geese floated.

"I'd say let's sit down," Jasper said, "but there doesn't appear to be anywhere that won't get us covered in poop."

Rob laughed and then pointed out a couple of markers across from the pond. "Would it be disrespectful to sit on a tombstone or two?"

Jasper shrugged. "Maybe, but I doubt anyone will complain."

Rob followed him to a couple of simple granite markers just off the road surrounding the pond. He let Jasper sit first and then sat down beside him.

"That got me, a little bit. What you said about Heather."

Jasper looked wistful, staring off into the endless blue of a horizon broken up by a very few cirrus clouds, up high. "Lacy," he said. "She wanted to be buried here." He glanced over at Rob. "But they took her away. To California."

Rob stared at the same blue sky, noticing how one of the clouds looked exactly like a bird in flight. He felt a strong pull *not* to talk about the young woman who had been, in the biological sense only, his daughter. She'd grown up seeing him as a beloved uncle. Until near the end of her life, that's what she'd believed.

And then the truth had come out.

But he didn't want to dwell on that. It made his stomach churn. Made him feel as though the contents of his room service breakfast might come up.

"Did you bring me here for any special reason? I mean, it's beautiful and all. Historic. But I have to admit, I never would have guessed—"

Jasper interrupted. "I know it seems strange, in light of what's happened, but this is a place of peace for me, not sadness. I like to think Lacy is here, her spirit anyway. It's where she wanted to be. She told me as much."

Rob nodded. There was no way he could make things any better—his brother and sister-in-law had wanted her close, and that meant there was never a moment when they considered a Chicago burial. He'd suggested it, even if it was a weak, soft-spoken push. He wished he'd been firmer, especially now that he knew for sure how important Chicago had been to her.

"It's interesting, don't you think?"

Rob smiled and nodded. "Why does it give you peace?"

And Jasper drew into himself. He was quiet for a long time, long enough for more clouds to gather on the horizon, at last blocking out the sun and reneging on its promise. In the wake of Jasper's silence, the day grew gray. The temperature dropped.

But he hadn't forgotten Rob's question. "It gives me peace because I like to think of loved ones here, not so much their bodies, because to be honest I don't actually know anyone who's buried here. But their spirits, which I don't think have to be hampered by the physical limitations we have in life. It makes me happy to think they're at peace, that they're resting. And the people who *are* here? It's wonderful that they had loved ones who cared so much they wanted to build something to memorialize them."

Jasper fell silent again. When he spoke once more, there were tears in his eyes. "I lost my mom and sister when I was a little kid."

Rob took Jasper's hand and squeezed it. He started to pull away, but Rob held fast.

"I don't like to talk about it, for many reasons. People think it's because it's too painful to bring up. But that's not it. That's not what it ever was. I was too young. I don't even remember my mom or the little sister I had, or the one on the way." Jasper eyed Rob. "Mom was pregnant when she was murdered."

Rob tensed at the mention of murder. Jasper had all these layers he could have never begun to guess at.

"Murdered? What happened?"

Jasper shook his head. "I've seen the papers from the time, and the bare bones of what happened is this." Jasper began to tell the tale.

Rob watched Jasper's face as he unemotionally laid out the story of how his mother, baby sister, and his mother's unborn child were all brutally murdered one quiet summer day in a used-furniture store in the small Illinois town where Jasper grew up. Save for the ever-changing shadows on Jasper's face, he revealed little, although his gaze took on a faraway aspect. That part wasn't surprising. The murders seemed as horrendous as those of the Clutter family in Truman Capote's *In Cold Blood*.

When Jasper finished, Rob asked him, "And did they catch who did it?"

"No. The owner of the store was killed at the same time. It was a quiet day. Hot. And you have to understand how small Haddonfield's downtown was. No one saw or heard a thing." Jasper laughed, but it was mirthless. "Such a huge, tragic thing—four lives, really, brutally snuffed out and not a witness to be found. People in town believe that someone, probably right in town, knows who the killer or killers were, but they won't come forward. Maybe it was a family member, someone they loved. Maybe they disappeared after they did what they did, and if someone knows, they just don't see the point in coming forward." Jasper shrugged. "Who knows? And I can't guess. There's, of course, a lot of wild speculation, which I don't even feel like going into, even though I know it might excite your Michael Blake alter ego, with your dips into dark suspense."

Rob shook his head, a little appalled. "No. It's not like that, Jasper. Not at all."

Jasper nodded. "What I remember most about that day is the neighbors."

"The neighbors? Why?"

"I remember being with Louise. She lived next door, and she and I were great friends." Jasper gave a little snort of laughter. "She might have been my *only* friend. Most of the other boys didn't want to be associated with the 'sensitive' boy who liked to read and, if the truth came out, played with Barbies."

Jasper sighed. "After what happened, Louise sort of stepped in and raised me. You couldn't find a kinder soul. But when I was a little boy, even before what happened, I was more likely to be found in her kitchen than out on a baseball field or something." Jasper tugged at a dandelion at his feet and brought it up to his face, where it cast a bit of yellow on his features. He held it as he continued. "The fact that I was the neighborhood sissy never mattered to Louise. She was always happy to see me. We gossiped. We watched old movies together. She taught me how to bake.

"It wasn't so odd that I was with her that day. I could have gone out with my mom and little sister. I don't remember it, but my dad says my mom even came next door that morning to take me with her to the furniture store." Jasper stopped suddenly, his mouth hanging open.

"What?"

"I just remembered why they were there. The old man who owned the store also owned a bunch of houses around town. From what I've heard, they were pretty run-down places, so he was kind of a slumlord. But he must have had a good one on offer because I think what she was doing at the store that day was she wanted to talk to him about a house. A home for us all. What with the new baby coming, the little two-bedroom we were in wouldn't have been enough. Hell, it probably wasn't enough even when it was just us.

"Anyway, I think she did go over to Louise's to grab me and take me with her. And Louise and I must have been playing Yahtzee or something. Maybe watching *Madame X* on some afternoon matinee show. I don't remember."

Jasper closed his eyes. "God, if I had gone with her..." He let the chilling thought hang in the quiet air. Over on Peterson Avenue, outside the cemetery, a noisy motorcycle raced by.

"She was kind of a guardian angel, Louise was," Rob said.

"Amen to that. You don't know the half of it." Jasper scratched for a moment behind one ear. "Getting back to where I was, though. It was the neighbors I remember. See, at some point a police car pulled up to our house and took my dad away. That was pretty scary for me, and I can vaguely remember Louise trying to calm me down, to reassure me that he wasn't in any trouble. I wonder sometimes if she knew what had happened and was being strong for me.

"Anyway, the neighbors. One by one, as the news started to spread, people began showing up on Louise's front porch. It was a big front porch, overlooking First Avenue and the service station across from her. There was a swing, chairs, a metal glider.

"People came and sat silently with us. One after the other, until the porch was full of neighborhood people. No one knocked. There may have been a small murmur of conversation, but the reason this sticks out so clearly in my mind, in my little boy memory, is that it was so quiet, and I wondered why no one was coming in.

"You see, they all knew by then. News like that traveled quickly, especially in a town the size of Haddonfield."

Jasper blinked as a couple of tears slid down his cheeks.

"They were all there for me," he said in a voice barely above a whisper. "They were all waiting to see how the little boy who was suddenly left without a mom and sister was.

"I don't know if I talked to them. I don't know if anyone even hugged me. I do remember Louise leaning close to speak with them in a hushed voice. I remember the sadness in her brown eyes when she took me back inside, closing the door behind her.

"She didn't tell. Not that day. All she did say was that I was spending the night with her and Jessie, her husband. And that she was going to make me my favorite supper—fried chicken, mashed potatoes and gravy, and corn on the cob, with apple pie for dessert."

Jasper stared down at the ground. After a long time, he finally looked back at Rob and smiled. He stretched.

"That talk of fried chicken and apple pie has made me hungry. What do you say we go get some lunch?"

Rob hadn't been sure what words he could offer that might temper the horrible memory Jasper had shared with him, so, only to himself, he had to admit he was relieved by the change of subject. Perhaps later the right words would come to him, as they did as he sat in front of a blank computer screen so many mornings, but for now, eating lunch seemed like a perfect idea.

He stood up. "I bet you have just the place in mind."

Jasper stood next to him, brushing the dust off his butt. "I do. I do indeed. You okay with a hippie joint? It's not far from here."

And even though Rob had no idea what a hippie joint would be like and suspected Jasper knew even less, he was intrigued.

And glad their day would be continuing.

*

"So I take it this place has been around for a long time?"

Rob sat with Jasper on the covered patio of a restaurant called the Amber Waves Café. The place looked like it had stepped out of a time warp from the late 1960s. It had this homespun, crunchy granola, run-down hippie vibe—and the food was organic and incredible. It was a couple of miles from the cemetery, but Jasper again had insisted they walk, in spite of the way the day had changed from sunny and clear to overcast with a promise of rain later. The smell of rain was in the air. Rob was surprised he could still detect that aroma, even after years and years of desert living.

They'd had lunch, bison chili for Rob and a BLT for Jasper, made with seitan bacon.

Rob had pointed to the sandwich. "Is that any good? You a vegetarian?"

"Yes, it is good. And no, I'm not." Jasper took a bite of the sandwich and washed it down with his Happy Heart, a juice blend of apple, carrot, ginger, and parsley.

"This was Lacy's favorite thing on the menu. I guess ordering it makes me feel a little closer to her. She'd approve. She and I would come here a lot. Many a Saturday morning, you'd find us here nursing hangovers and eating pancakes." He smiled. "She was a vegetarian, but you knew that, right?"

Rob didn't answer. He didn't know. He supposed there were a lot of things he didn't know about his own daughter—especially changes that had come about in the recent past. But he didn't want to talk about his deficiencies. Instead, he commented on how amazing his bison chili was. The truth nagged at him—for the last couple of years or so of her life, Heather, or Lacy, hadn't spoken to him. Moving to Chicago had been her way of asserting her independence. But, it had also been a means by which to punish him and the people she'd once thought of as her parents.

He stared down into his beer. He'd always thought there'd be time to mend fences, to repair the damage. *We never know, do we, when the old clock will run out?* He smiled sadly at Jasper. "What are we gonna do next?"

Jasper gave him a pointed look. "You're avoiding talking about her. That's okay. I get it. But we will, sooner or later." He pointed first at Rob and then at himself and said, "But this—you and me—can't really progress too far if we don't discuss her. I know we both loved her."

Rob nodded and said quietly, "We will. Can it just wait until a little later, though?" He shrugged and heat rose in his cheeks. "It's really painful for me." He left it there. He could have added, "Especially when you consider the role I might have played in her suicide," but he was unable to mouth the words. They would be like an arrow to his heart.

Rob hurriedly finished his chili and grabbed their waitress as she passed. He handed her a credit card and asked her to tally their bill.

She walked away. Jasper frowned. "Lunch was going to be my treat."

"How about you buy me dinner?" Rob cocked an eyebrow at Jasper.

"Fair enough. You like Ethiopian food?"

"I can honestly say I don't think I've had it."

"I'll take you to another one of my favorite places. Today is all about favorite places. For me. For Lacy. I want you to know the woman I knew because I don't think she was quite the girl you kept in your heart."

Rob nodded. "I think you're right. So where do we go from here, Jasper? What place do you want to show me through Heather's—" He stopped and corrected himself. "—through Lacy's eyes?"

Jasper stood. "You'll see."

Rob signed the Visa receipt the waitress brought over, giving her a tip about equal to the amount of the bill. He stood next to Jasper. "Can we please ride to this next place? My poor dogs!" Rob was thinking a cab or an Uber Black. Something comfortable.

A rumble almost drowned out his words, and Jasper smiled. "The Morse L stop is right across the street."

Chapter Thirteen

The L ride was short, only one stop until Jarvis.

As Jasper rose to exit, Rob grabbed his shoulder, confused. "You got to be kidding me. We could have walked this."

"You said you wanted to ride. Come on." Jasper led him off the train onto the wooden platform between the tracks. Jarvis was the stop closest to his apartment on Fargo Avenue, so Jasper was very familiar with it—it almost felt like home. The station always smelled like urine to Jasper, and for some perverse reason, he was proud to share that with Rob. He thought the scent might broaden his elitist horizons.

Rob followed him down the stairs to the street. As he descended, Jasper recalled ascending those same stairs with Lacy close behind. They were scrambling to catch the train that was already in the station. It had been winter then, bitter cold, and the platform was icy. Just as they got to the top, Jasper slipped and hit his head on the wooden covering for the stairs. It had hurt and left a quickly rising goose egg, but Lacy had alternated between laughter and making sympathetic faces all the way to Boystown, where they were headed for yet another night of revelry in the bars along Halsted Street. Jasper could hear the tinkle of her laughter now.

He didn't recount this adventure to Rob. It seemed private—belonging only to Lacy and him. Sometimes,

Jasper thought, it was things being known to two people that made them special.

Outside on Jarvis, the dark clouds that had threatened rain were now making good on their promise.

Jasper gave Rob what he knew was an evil grin. "So our walk now is only about as long as the L ride we just took."

Jasper couldn't help but burst into laughter when Rob groaned as he looked up at the sky where lightning flashed, followed by an almost deafening thunderclap. "You know we could turn around and go back to the Four Seasons? Raid the minibar. Order room service. I think there's two of those fluffy robes..."

"But the Four Seasons wasn't one of Lacy's favorite places. She would have said it was 'hopelessly and helplessly bourgeois.' Whatever that means." Jasper didn't know why he added the last part. He knew exactly what she'd meant. Now, knowing what he did about her and her background, he could identify, if not understand, her pronounced contempt for the upper class.

"So, we're walkin' somewhere?" Rob asked, leaning back against the wall of the train station. "I don't have an umbrella." It was dirty under the tracks, and it smelled. Litter and pigeon shit desecrated the sidewalk.

"Will you melt if you get wet?" Jasper asked.

"My beautiful wickedness!" Rob said and laughed.

Jasper wondered, *Should I give him a break? Should we just go back to his hotel? Or at least wait out the downpour in the café down the street? A latte does sound good about now...*

But no, the plan is to take him to Lacy's favorite places. It was a plan that had only gradually come together, on the fly. The fact that it was raining would nake the plan better. Lacy was the kind of woman who oved to frolic in the rain. He saw her in his mind's eye, one dusky night not long after they met, dancing in her black dress and Stevie Nicks black lacy shawl at the end of the pier at Ardmore Beach, the gay beach. There was no one around, and Jasper remembered how she looked, her goth makeup running down her face, her clothes plastered to her body, black hair ropy and free.

She'd been beautiful.

Jasper took Rob's hand. "Let's go." He pulled him out from under the L tracks and into the cold downpour. They both gasped as the first drops hit them.

"How far?" Rob shouted over grumbling thunder.

"Half a mile, tops." And Jasper tugged harder so that they ran east down Jarvis Avenue.

"That far? Seriously?" Rob cried.

"Buck up. Be a man! Once we're drenched, we're drenched. You won't feel it as much."

"If you say so," Rob mumbled. Jasper barely heard him.

*

Jasper tried to experience the view through Rob's eyes but ended up seeing it through Lacy's instead. They stood at the top of a flight of broad concrete stairs leading down to Fargo Avenue beach. Jasper had not let go of Rob's hand the whole five or six blocks it took to get there. The heat of his palm against Jasper's, contrasted with the damp, chilly air, was sensual and caused Jasper's pulse to rise, surprisingly.

The beach stretched out in full a little to the south. Right below them was a thin strip of sand, pebbles, and bigger rocks. The water, pockmarked with rain and pewter colored, rolled into the shoreline with fury, bashing itself against the rocks at the shore so hard geysers of spray shot up as though projected from a blowhole. An island of boulders a little offshore rose up out of the water. Jasper and Lacy, on end-of-summer days when Lake Michigan's temperature went from icy to barely tolerable, would wade and then swim the few feet out to it and bask in the sun there, like seals. He could see her in his mind's eye in cutoff shorts and a black T-shirt knotted above her waist.

Jasper had told the truth as they started out in the rain—once thoroughly soaked, one didn't feel the cold and the shock of it as much anymore. Being drenched became a natural state, and the body gave up its shock and outrage and went along. At least that's how it was for Jasper; he hoped the same was true for Rob.

He glanced over at him and was relieved to see that at least Rob wasn't shivering.

"What do you think?" Jasper asked. The rain had slowed to a steady downpour. The air was infused with its scent, which Jasper thought was beautiful, especially when combined with the freshwater, slightly fishy smell of the lake. There was also a stillness to the air, almost as if the world were holding its breath.

Rob surprised him. He tugged at Jasper's hand. "Let's go down to the beach."

Jasper let him lead the way down the broad steps. There was something about this moment, Jasper thought, that possessed a kind of magic. Their intertwined and interlocked fingers. The wet of their skin. The gray skies and heavy, close-to-the-horizon clouds. The chill in the air. The distant flash of lightning across the broad plain of churning water. Feeling safe with this man...

A sudden thought came to him. *Why didn't you tell him Louise had passed?* He wondered if it was because it was too much, or maybe he was still processing the loss. The grief waited for him, like a wraith in the corner.

They were the only ones on the beach. Jasper wasn't surprised because it was, after all, a weekday, and a rainy one at that. But still... Chicago was a huge metropolis, with millions of people living west of the roiling blue-gray waters of Lake Michigan. You'd think, even in the rain, someone would be out here, with a dog maybe.

Jasper told himself not to look a gift horse in the mouth and to take advantage of this moment of solitude and togetherness while it lasted. He knew it wouldn't— someone was sure to come along.

They headed to the water's edge, where Rob surprised him again. He stooped down to take off his shoes and roll up his pant legs. Perhaps the man wasn't as unadventurous as Jasper thought. Perhaps the desert dweller had no idea of the icy chill of Lake Michigan's waters.

Jasper pointed to the pant legs and shook his head. "With these waves, do you really think you're going to keep your pants dry if you wade in?"

Without waiting for a response, Jasper made a move he knew he'd regret later. He walked into the water, thinking he was doing the right thing, the kind thing.

He squeezed his eyes shut and gasped. The water was so cold it was painful, as though a creature made of ice, with a thousand tiny teeth, was biting into him. It was, oddly, almost like the lick of flame. Jasper turned back to Rob, who still stood sensibly at the water's edge. Teeth chattering, Jasper managed to say, "Do. Not. Come. In."

He hurried back to Rob, pushing him away from the crashing surf. Freezing, he bear-hugged him, huddling against his body for the relative warmth it gave off.

And Rob hugged him back, holding him close in a way that Jasper knew wasn't only for protection from the elements.

Jasper felt encircled and hot in spite of the rain and his thoughtless and clueless wade into the arctic waters. He leaned back a little to look up at Rob, whose face was pale, slick with rainwater.

And that's when Rob leaned down and kissed him. Jasper shut his eyes, reveling in the heat from Rob's mouth, the slightly sweet taste of his tongue. He bit gently on Rob's lower lip. The kiss, with the slowly dying rain pouring down on them, was like no other Jasper had ever experienced. He wanted it to last forever.

And it might have had not a woman arrived with her dog.

They broke apart clumsily, reluctantly, as a panting presence began sniffing at their ankles. Jasper looked down to see a little mutt, fawn colored, undeterred by the rain, standing on his calf and looking up at him with warm brown eyes almost as though wondering where *his* kiss was. His curled tail wagged so hard it was a blur.

He must have been some kind of terrier-Chihuahua mix, because he was small but with legs long enough and ears huge enough to be comically endearing.

"Vito!" the woman shouted. "Get back here! Leave those boys alone."

Rob leaned into Jasper's ear to whisper, "She called us boys. Bless her heart."

The woman came up to them, a little breathless. She was probably fiftysomething, around Rob's age, with buzz-cut salt-and-pepper hair and a smile that lit up the gray day. "I am so sorry." She shooed Vito away from them, and he ran along the edge of the water, playing tag with the ebb and flow of the waves.

Her eyes, the color of dark chocolate, took them in from behind her silver cat-eye framed glasses. "Please don't tell me that was your first kiss." She let out a short bark of laughter.

Before either of them could respond, she waved a hand at them. "None of my business. But you might want to take it indoors—for a whole host of good reasons." The smile returned as she turned to walk away. She gave them a little wave over her shoulder as she started moving south, Vito running behind her.

Thunder rumbled as though to give one last dying breath, and then the rain suddenly went from a drizzle to nothing at all. Clouds shifted a bit to reveal a patch of blue sky.

"She's right, you know." Rob eyed Jasper. "Indoors sounds really good right about now. And you—with those wet shoes—must be freezing."

"Do you want to get inside?"

"I do. Very much." Rob grinned, enough to let Jasper know he'd picked up on the little double entendre.

"My place or yours?" Jasper asked. He knew his apartment a few blocks from them would be empty. Stan would be at work.

Rob pressed close. "You live nearby, right?"

Jasper nodded. "Come on."

*

When they opened the door to the apartment, Jasper took it in as though seeing it for the first time, as Rob was.

He was both pleased and a little embarrassed by th view. He didn't know he'd be having a visitor, so the plac wasn't exactly tidy. The fact was, he'd pretty mucl promised himself he *wouldn't* invite Rob home—not thi soon anyway. So much for good intentions!

He wished the apartment were cleaner. There was ai empty Popchips bag on the table, along with a now-gone flat glass of some purple-colored soft drink. The tabl surface wore a furry layer of dust. Inside the hearth of th decorative fireplace, Stan had stacked issues o *Entertainment Weekly* and a few empty boxes from gam software. A pair of Stan's shoes, loafers for Christ's sake lay between the couch and the coffee table. Jasper trie not to breathe it in, but the place had a faint odor c perspiration and something else, maybe corn chips? H shuddered.

In spite of all this, the little place did have its charm The hardwood floors gleamed. Washed-out sunlight cam in through the large windows facing Fargo Avenue outside of which one could take in the budding trees. Th crown molding and other vintage touches, like th frosted-glass wall sconces above the fireplace and built-i cabinetry, made the place feel homey and warm.

Warm in the metaphorical sense. "Shit. It's cold i here. You cold?" Jasper didn't wait for Rob to answe "Heat's included in the rent. But it's supposed to b springtime, you know? So they shut off the radiator about a week ago, regardless of the temperature. Gott love Chicago landlords and their cluelessness about loca weather. Spring in Chicago means freezing days, rain, an then, boom, heat and oppressive humidity. Hellc summer!"

"It's not so bad. And this place is really charming."

"Ah, come on. I've seen your house. Literally like something out of *Architectural Digest*."

"I probably shouldn't say this, but it has been featured there—before I bought the house, mind you." Rob wandered left, toward the dining room that had been converted into Jasper's bedroom.

Jasper gave out a little gasp as he hurried after him. "Sorry." He rushed to pull up the covers and smoothed them with a trembling hand. "So your place has been in a magazine and you're gonna pull my leg and tell me this hole is 'charming'?" Jasper chuckled. "Come on!"

"Yes, because it's you. I love the retro flavor of the place." Rob walked into the kitchen and eyed the old porcelain sink with the plaid skirt underneath and the walk-in pantry. He peered out the window of the back door to the big yard in the back, walled in by L tracks above. "It's so urban and at the same time homey."

"Are you patronizing me?"

"No, I'm serious!" Rob turned and checked the bathroom out next. He gave a low whistle. "That's an original porcelain claw-foot tub! Look how deep it is. And the way it reclines! You must love taking baths. They don't make tubs like that anymore, not even the luxury ones."

"Yeah, but look at the sink and its two handles, one for hot and one for cold. You can never have just warm water unless you fill up the basin."

Rob eyed him. "Can't you just take a compliment? Maybe appreciate what you have?"

Jasper's mouth dropped open. He thought he should be offended, but Rob's observation was spot-on. Why couldn't he let himself believe Rob found his home charming? It was. It really was. He knew it, so why couldn't he hear it from someone else?

Because Rob was rich?

Jasper remembered when he and Lacy had first seen the apartment, shown around by the building's property manager. They'd both loved it, the way the light streamed in, its spaciousness for a one-bedroom. Even its proximity to the L tracks, practically sitting on top of them, was quirky and kind of wonderful.

Jasper didn't know what to say, so he changed the subject. "I need to get into something dry. I'm going to freeze to death in this wet shit."

Rob nodded. He turned and walked into the living room. Jasper followed. "Grab a seat on the couch. I'll make some coffee after I get changed. That'll warm us up."

He veered around the corner into his own room and quickly stripped down, feeling irrationally modest for once in his life, and changed into a hoodie and a pair of red-and-white-checked flannel sleep pants. He noticed his bare feet were bright red from the freezing lake water and rain and thought he was lucky not to have frostbite. He retrieved a pair of faded sock-monkey socks from a drawer and pulled them on.

Jasper poked his head back into the living room. "I just have to heat the water up for the French press."

Rob nodded toward the closed door at the other end of the living room.

"Was that her room?"

Jasper caught his breath. It was almost as though Lacy might be behind the closed, white-painted wooden door, sleeping off a night of drinking. Oh, how he wished she was.

"Yeah. Of course."

Rob stood. "Can I see it? I mean, if your roommate wouldn't mind? I don't want to invade his privacy."

"I think it'll be okay," Jasper said softly. He moved to open the door, but something caused him to halt in his tracks. "You sure you want to do this? It was where she—" He let the unsaid hang in the air, like a wisp of smoke.

"I know," Rob said. "I'd still like to see."

Jasper moved to the door and placed his hand on the knob. "It's mostly Stan's room now. You're not gonna see a lot of her in there." He didn't mention that he'd donated her bed, dresser, and chest of drawers to the Brown Elephant, a thrift store over on Clark. He swung the door open, and for a moment, he saw her lying there, staring at him with her dark eyes and grinning.

The image vanished as quickly as it had come. "Sorry, Stan's even more of a slob than I am."

Rob walked into the room. He looked out the big window that faced Fargo and then the smaller one facing the L tracks. He opened the closet door and peeked inside the walk-in. Jasper could recall it being filled with black clothes.

"This was where she ended up?" Rob asked, like he couldn't believe it.

Jasper had never known that Lacy was a daughter of wealth and privilege. He'd always assumed, and she'd never corrected him, that they both came from humble working-class backgrounds.

"Yup," Jasper said, a little annoyed, assuming that Rob was marveling at how far down she'd tumbled.

Rob looked over his shoulder at him. "I'm sorry. I didn't mean that to come out like it sounded." He stood, hands at his sides, and Jasper thought suddenly that Rob looked a little lost, a little helpless. "Was she happy here?"

"I thought so." Did he? Did he really? Or did he not pay any mind to her despair? To the fact that she had no friends and worked at a job far below her education or intellectual capacity? Was it easier to use her as a sounding board, a wingperson, a shoulder to cry on listening ears when he needed them? Had he ever thought to reciprocate? Suddenly, he wanted to cry. But he held it back, the lump in his throat like a tangerine lodged there.

"No," Jasper finally said. "I don't know if she was happy." Obviously, she wasn't all that happy. He hung his head, staring down at the dust bunnies gathered on the floor.

"We didn't know much about what was happening with her." Rob turned and made to move toward the door. "I mean, of course we knew where she was, that she was safe, that she was getting along. But she didn't speak to us, didn't answer calls, emails, texts. Unlike almost everyone else in the world, she had no social-media presence." Rob drew in a breath. "It was like she vanished."

Although a bit of sun had come out, it was as though a pall of darkness had descended upon them.

"And you have no idea why," Jasper said. It wasn't a question.

"Did you say you were going to make coffee?"

Relieved, Jasper led him from the room, shutting the door after them. "I did. I think we have cream and sugar."

"That's okay. I take mine like my heart—black." Rob laughed, but the mirth didn't reach his eyes.

Jasper started for the kitchen, but he turned for one more look at Rob. When he saw him sitting there on the couch, with the diffused light hitting his face just so and casting dramatic shadows, a play of light and dark, he turned back and sat down beside him again. Rob moved closer to Jasper on the couch. "Would it be weird if I kissed you here?"

"You mean here?" Jasper pointed to the tip of his nose. "Or here?" He lifted a foot and wiggled his big toe. "Or really weird if you kissed me here?" He caressed the back of a knee.

Rob smirked. "You know what I mean. Here in this room."

"Ah—gotcha. I suppose it's as good a place as any, but I have to warn you that Stan will be home in a couple of hours."

"I think I can finish a kiss in that time frame." Rob touched Jasper's cheek. "Maybe." He leaned in, and as his face drew near, Jasper sucked in a breath. There had been many such moments with many men late at night on this very couch, so why did this one seem different? Why did this one seem important, charged with a kind of giddy energy?

When their lips met, it was almost as though he'd touched some of the lightning they'd witnessed on the beach. Because his eyes were closed, he imagined sparks flying out from their merged lips.

It didn't take long for desire to surge upward, like one of those waves they'd just seen down on Fargo Avenue beach. The hunger rose like a wave far out from land, building higher and higher as it closed in until it crashed against the shore with furious spray.

When they finally broke apart, Jasper was breathless and almost whimpering with a yearning he'd forgotten how to feel, what with all of the perfunctory one-night stands and online hookups in his recent past. Or maybe he'd never known what love and sexual desire really felt like, what a potent cocktail they made when combined, especially with someone new.

Had his mind allowed the word *love* to manifest?

Never mind. He returned to kissing Rob, moving on from his lips to his neck, his eyebrows, and his earlobes. When he descended farther south, he pulled away only long enough to say, "Take off your shirt."

Quickly and wordlessly, Rob complied, allowing Jasper to concentrate on his broad, hairy chest, the nipples that protruded like pencil erasers. Jasper found himself lost in the taste and texture of Rob's skin, attuned to the sound of his breathing, quickening, interspersed with what Jasper interpreted as involuntary groans of pleasure. His tongue circled a surprise—a heavy silver ring pierced into Rob's left nipple. He tugged at it with his teeth, causing Rob to moan.

Jasper allowed his hand to wander down to Rob's crotch. He found him fully hard, and Jasper chastised himself for being surprised—Rob wasn't *that* much older that Jasper should have anticipated anything less.

It was clear the time was right to make a suggestion. "Should we move into my bedroom?" he managed to get out beneath his hurried breaths.

"I thought we were gonna have coffee. You promised me coffee," Rob said.

Jasper leaned back to eye him, to gauge if he was serious or not. There was a twinkle in Rob's eye. His lips quivered in an almost repressed laugh.

"Later. Now I need something more." Jasper pulled Rob up from the couch.

"I thought your roomie was coming home from work any minute now." Rob followed, grinning.

"We have at least an hour or two. And sweetie, this isn't gonna take nearly that long." Jasper tugged at the waistband of his bottoms to allow his erection to pop free. "Somebody needs release...bad."

Rob gave a low whistle. He squeezed Jasper's dick, which caused Jasper to shudder and jerk. "You didn't tell me you were hung like a horse."

"Oh shut up. Flattery will get you everywhere."

"I hope wherever that is, I can ride there with that up my butt," Rob said, but he wasn't smiling. His gaze was now only directed at Jasper's cock.

Jasper felt like a piece of meat.

Something to be used.

And he didn't mind a bit.

He tugged Rob along behind him, knowing there was no need for it. At this point, Rob would have followed him anywhere, overcoming even the most powerful obstacles.

Together, they collapsed on the bed. Jasper was grateful he hadn't bothered to make it that morning.

In minutes, he was deep inside Rob, Rob's legs on his shoulders. Jasper had predicted he wouldn't last long, and he didn't.

When he finished and had pulled out, he yanked the condom from his deflating dick and drizzled the come all over Rob's chest and belly. The sight, smell, and feel of his seed must have had the desired effect because, without touching himself at all, Rob shot arcs of come so huge they hit the headboard over his head.

Jasper collapsed on top of him, gasping. Their bodies were fused together with come and sweat.

"Next time, we'll take our time," Rob whispered in Jasper's ear, then bit the lobe.

"Who said there's going to be a next time?" Jasper asked. "That's awfully presumptuous! Now that I've fucked you, I need you to get the hell out of here. I have things to do today." He tapped an imaginary watch on his wrist. "Time's a-wastin'!"

Rob eyed him. His lips were open in a little moue of uncertainty.

"You think I'm kidding?" Jasper sat up and began to clean the come from himself with the sheet. He stood naked and walked to the window, where the rumble of an L train racing by could be heard beyond the shut mini blinds. "You need to get your ass dressed and get out of here." He turned and looked at Rob, lying prone on the bed.

He'd never seen a sight so beautiful.

"Are you serious?" Rob asked. There was a little quaver in his voice.

"What do you think?" Jasper hopped back on the bed, and an errant touch of his skin against Rob's had him hard again.

The next time took a bit longer, and Jasper was delighted it was so close on the heels of the first time.

They fell asleep in each other's arms. Jasper dreamed of making coffee and serving it to Rob in bed. The dream was so vivid and real that when he did awaken, to the sound of a key being fitted into the front-door lock, he wondered if the moment had actually happened.

He looked up from Rob's chest at his damp and bespectacled roommate, squinting at the two of them on the bed. Jasper groped for the comforter and pulled it up, covering their nakedness.

"Hey," Stan said. He disappeared from view, followed by the sound of his bedroom door opening and closing.

"That was my roommate," he said to Rob.

"I hoped so. I didn't want to share you with anyone."

The thought made Jasper laugh until Rob put finger to his lips. "We need to get you dressed. The Four Seasons awaits us."

"I hear they have good room service there."

"They do. Come on," Rob nudged him.

Chapter Fourteen

"We're taking an Uber to the Four Seasons. I've had enough of the L for one day. Please show me some kindness," Rob said, laughing.

Allow the guy a little mercy. You know yourself that riding the L can be a peculiar, smelly kind of hell. Besides, after looking out the window to see the rain had started up again—hard and relentless, the sky heavy with clouds and closer to night than day—Jasper had to concede the ride south in a warm, heated car occupied by only the two of them in the back seat sounded awfully fine.

They emerged from his apartment building to hurry to the waiting black Lexus. Jasper thought suddenly of the man who'd picked him up in front of Carltons on Clark one cold winter night. What was his name? Jerry? He could see him in his mind's eye and recalled how trepidation had turned to grudging appreciation for the man who bore an uneasy resemblance to John Wayne Gacy. Jerry had told him to find fireworks while he was still young.

And almost as if on cue, the sky lit up with a brilliant streak of lightning, so bright it hurt his eyes. The thunderclap that immediately followed was so loud it hurt his ears and set off car alarms on the street.

There was a sharp tang of ozone in the chilly air.

He clutched on to Rob. "Wow."

Rob said nothing for a moment, then turned to Jasper. "I felt the earth move. Did you?"

Jasper smiled as the car pulled smoothly away from the curb. "Earlier I did."

"That's what I was talking about," Rob whispered.

The driver, a middle-aged man with thinning red hair and freckles, eyed them in the rearview mirror with bloodshot blue eyes. Jasper snuggled closer to Rob, who put an arm around him.

At first, Jasper thought the driver was appalled, but then he broke into a grin. He took one last look at them in the mirror and sighed, "Young love."

Truer words, Jasper thought, *truer words...*

*

Traffic was bad all the way downtown, especially on Lake Shore Drive. Jasper had witnessed it before—a little rain and drivers went nuts, suddenly losing any skills behind the wheel they'd once possessed.

The only saving grace was that he was in this warm little bubble with Rob. Rain smeared the windows, and the driver had set the heat to just the right temperature. He had his music tuned to something classical and soothing.

Jasper fell asleep on Rob's shoulder somewhere in between his apartment and the Four Seasons.

He was in Louise's kitchen, sitting, as they always would, at her maple kitchen table. Jasper stuffed his face with a huge piece of Louise's homemade sweet-potato pie.

Louise watched him, sipping coffee, the steam from which would obscure her entire face when she lifted it close to her lips.

*"You know that man's gonna be good for you, huh?"
The steam cleared as she set the mug back down.*

His mouth full, Jasper could only nod and attempt a smile.

He looked up as he heard the floor creak. Lacy stepped into the room. She wore a pair of black leather pants paired with a simple cotton men's button-down shirt, also in black. Her dark hair tied back from her face, she wore no makeup, and this fact made her look younger, almost innocent. Jasper swallowed, staring up at her, lingering there in the archway between Louise's kitchen and dining room.

Louise looked over at her. "I like your hair that way. Shows off that pretty face."

Jasper shivered. "You're both dead."

And they both burst into laughter.

Rob was shaking him. "Jasper? We're here."

Jasper felt disoriented as the car pulled up in front of the Four Seasons. A uniformed bellman hurried over, umbrella raised, to protect them from the rain.

Clutching Rob's arm, Jasper hurried inside.

He tried to shake the dream as they passed through the lobby full of people and headed upstairs in one of the silent elevators, their only companion a small woman, in a lavender skirt and tan sweater set, who put him in mind of Judi Dench.

Once in the room, Rob gestured toward the couch. "Have a seat. I never did get that coffee, so I'm going to order some room service. You want anything to eat?"

"Now that you mention it, I'm starving."

Rob raised an eyebrow. "We both worked up an appetite." He groped around on the desk and handed Jasper the room service menu. "Tell me what you want."

I want Lacy back. I want a relationship with my dad. I want to talk to Louise at her kitchen table just one more time, to be sure she knows how much I love her. The words sprouted automatically in Jasper's mind, but he didn't utter them. He was surprised at how they came to him, at him, so quickly. He bowed his head to peruse the menu, pressing a finger to his lips. He pretended to be in earnest thought to try to regain his composure. It took him a moment for his eyes to focus on the print in front of him.

"How about the salmon? And some french fries? And some of the flourless chocolate cake?"

Rob took the menu back. "A man after my own heart." He called down and ordered everything Jasper had requested, along with a bottle of champagne and a large carafe of coffee.

"Will we really eat any of this stuff?" Jasper wondered. He was already eager to get out of the damp jogging pants and Under Armour hoodie he'd donned before leaving the apartment.

"Of course we will. Because we're civilized. Not animals. And it's our duty to rise above our baser impulses, even if it's only to eat." He tapped Jasper's knee. "I need sustenance before round three. Humor an old man."

"Who said there was going to be a round three?" Jasper grinned. "And I don't see any old men in this room."

"Stop." Rob glanced out the window at the Chicago skyline. It was getting dark, and the lights in the urban towers had come on, making of the high-rises illuminated towers, magical. Jasper wondered what would happen next, where they would go once the food was eaten and another round of orgasms was complete. Would he return to his humble—and humdrum—life? Would Rob simply jet back to Palm Springs and never give him a second thought? Would Jasper endure incredulous laughs in his face if he dared mention his dalliance with big-time author Michael Blake?

Because, you know, this can't last. He's out of your league. That shopboy with his own little studio apartment and maybe, if he's lucky, beater car, is out here somewhere, waiting for you to complete him. You'll meet, have out-of-control sex, fall in love, move in together in your apartment or his, and finally save up enough together to buy a small condo. You'll get a dog from the Humane Society. You'll vacation across the lake in Saugatuck. Camping. You'll grow old together. It will be okay.

This man is too good for you.

*

They ate. They drank half the bottle of champagne. They ignored the coffee, but gorged on the cake. They drank the other half of the bottle after the cake, sometimes transferring the fizzy elixir from one mouth to another, following that up with a passionate kiss. It felt like a scene from some romantic-comedy movie.

And when it was all done, they fell together on the bed, stomachs full, slightly dizzy.

Jasper rolled over and bussed Rob on the cheek. "Did anyone ever tell you you're the sexiest man alive?" And he meant it. Rob might have been twice his age, but Jasper felt in no way deprived. The silver of his hair, the salt-and-pepper stubble on the sharp planes of his jawline, the strong Roman nose, and the warmth in those eyes—

infinite—caused Jasper's heart to fill with both love and lust.

"Are you too full?" Jasper asked.

"Too full for what?"

"Anything. Reciprocating. I haven't felt you inside me yet." Jasper toyed with the top button of Rob's jeans.

Rob removed Jasper's hand. Softly, he said, "Let's take this slow, okay?" He rose to undress quickly while Jasper watched, noticing with satisfaction his cock already standing above half-mast. He turned to move across the room and pull the draperies closed. He snapped off the two table lamps in the room to plunge it into an almost pitchy darkness.

Jasper, without getting up, without even sitting up, wriggled out of his clothes and kicked them to the floor. He lay on his back, reminding himself to breathe. Rob fumbled around in the dark.

He must have stubbed a toe because he uttered a curse and then, mysteriously, "Aha! Here they are."

With a snick and flare of a match, Rob lit two candles in frosted-glass holders, lighting his face eerily from below. The flames' illumination danced across the ceiling, making shadows caper.

Jasper could say nothing, only open his arms as Rob neared him. When he weighed down his side of the bed and, at last, moved on top of Jasper so that their two bodies became one, Jasper finally allowed a breath, in the form of a moan, to escape.

"You're all I ever wanted," Rob said. He pulled back slightly, as though surprised at his own admission, but then Jasper conceded that maybe it was only to take a good look at him before he leaned in for a kiss.

The kiss was the first of many—long, short, rapturous, rough as sandpaper, gentle as the touch of a butterfly wing, here, there, everywhere.

In the midst of the caresses, the licks, and the bites, Jasper lost track of time, of space, of everything. He didn't think it was because of the champagne.

*

When Jasper awakened hours later, it was to more thunder and a barely diffuse light pervading the room. At some point, Rob must have risen to open the draperies. The candles still flickered but threw off a stronger scent—jasmine, maybe. Mandarin orange? He shifted a little to slide off of Rob's chest.

Rob snored, and there was a little line of drool at the corner of his lips. Rather than being repelled, Jasper thought it was adorable.

At Jasper's movement, though, Rob's eyelids fluttered open. "Is it morning?"

"Nah. It's raining again, though. Pouring."

"I'm not used to rain," Rob said. "How do you all stand it?"

Jasper turned on his back and chuckled. "What? It doesn't rain where you live?"

"Hardly ever."

"Seriously?"

"Seriously. It's the desert, sweetheart. Water there is a rare and wonderful thing."

Jasper fell silent for a while, listening to the rain's lashes against the windows. It sounded like needles, and Jasper wondered if there wasn't some snow mixed in. Even though it was spring, anything could happen in Chicago.

He finally gave voice to the question he dreaded asking because the answer could be much more complicated than it might appear on the surface. "So...when do you need to go back?" He shifted. "To the desert?"

Rob shrugged. "Maybe never."

The answer stunned Jasper. *He has to be kidding.*

"Maybe I'll just stay here. With you." And he turned and kissed Jasper—long, luxuriously. A flame could have been ignited, but Jasper, for once in his young and perpetually horny life, wanted to talk. In bed. With a hot man.

What was happening to him?

Jasper didn't even want to fantasize about how that might work. Still, his mind ran to a penthouse with Lincoln Park, lake, and city views. He and Rob curled up on an oversized sofa with two Italian greyhounds curled at their feet. He thought of accompanying Rob on book tours, the quiet but proud guy in the background as hordes of fans crowded the signing table, jockeying for position for coveted chairs at a reading.

"You wouldn't do that," Jasper said.

"Why not?" Rob smiled. "I can do whatever I want."

"Must be nice to have money." Jasper wanted to force the words back in his mouth.

Rob didn't seem to mind. Maybe he was used to the mention of money—or the envy of it.

"People say money can't buy happiness, but it does give me freedom. And it certainly provides the solution to a lot of problems, both real and potential." Rob stared up at the ceiling. "Look, I've always been rich. I don't say that to brag, but it's just a fact of life. Does that bother you?" He turned a bit to face Jasper.

"A little." Jasper rubbed his eyes and then laughed self-consciously. "No. A lot. Unlike you, I grew up poor...in a two-bedroom house that probably had the square footage of this suite. We ate things like boxed macaroni and cheese and fish sticks. If Dad was feeling extravagant, he might spring for a round steak. One of my favorite breakfasts is frozen waffles with fried Spam."

Rob laughed.

"You think I'm kidding? I ate so much of that crap growing up that whenever I see a blue can, I start to salivate. People think it's nasty, but it actually is pretty good, probably because it's loaded with salt.

"Anyway, I think being poor made me suspicious of rich people. The unfairness of them having so much when I had so little."

"Unless we're really destitute, we all have the same stuff—food, a roof over our heads, someone to love us, maybe."

"Easy for you to say."

"True for me to say."

They fell silent for the longest time. Jasper wondered if Rob had drifted back to sleep. His own eyes were fluttering when Rob spoke again.

"Lacy had money."

Jasper turned a little. "What?"

"Heather. Lacy. She was a daughter of privilege. She grew up with everything she wanted. Went to exclusive private schools. Equestrian lessons. The best toys, the best clothes, the best shoes. A cute little Infiniti for her sweet sixteen." Rob's face was flickering pain and nostalgia. Jasper assumed the memories were coming now. And he had no idea what the texture, the shape, of those memories would be. He didn't know this girl.

"What did she look like?" Jasper asked, because he really didn't know.

Rob's answer surprised him. "Thin, blonde, the silkiest, straightest hair that hung down to her waist. A California girl."

Jasper almost laughed because the description of Lacy was so far afield from the young woman he had known and loved. But he didn't laugh. The description foreign and strange, ultimately made him sad.

"That's *not* her. She wasn't like that at all." His Lacy was dark. Sure, they had laughs sometimes. And their nights out and pub crawls were legendary. Jasper recalled being at some piano bar with her one late night and Lacy going over backward in her seat at their bistro table, her head landing in the lap of the guy behind her. She wasn't motivated to move. The guy behind her was most decidedly not amused. He remembered that night was a sick pain—the long walk through the streets of Wicker Park, searching for a cab. Jasper had had to help her up off the sidewalk more than once. He remembered the long days and nights when she wouldn't get out of bed, when she would simply lie there, doing nothing, staring at the wall.

Why didn't I do more to help?

Her hair, her clothes, so decidedly not blonde, no colorful, reflected her. She liked to joke that she had a black heart, a black soul. But the joke fell flat when you realized how depressed she was. Jasper felt a hot flush of shame that he didn't truly absorb the truth of that until it was too late.

"What happened to her?" he asked Rob, his voice weak, breath trembly.

Rob said nothing for a long time. Finally, he rolled onto his back and stared up at the ceiling. Maybe he was watching the flickering shadows. Maybe he was simply thinking. "You really want to know?"

"More than anything," Jasper said. He moved so that his head rested on Rob's chest.

Chapter Fifteen

"The trouble started a few years ago, on one of Heather's birthdays," Rob said. "I'd gone out to Indian Wells to her house for a party her mom was throwing. It was one of those gatherings that Heather had come to despise almost as much as I did. See, my sister-in-law was about one thing and one thing only—impressing people.

"So the birthday party had little to do with Heather, really. It was about showing off for her friends. Heather's mom came from Vegas, literally trailer trash. And I'm sorry to say that, but it was true. I think marrying into money was a two-edged sword. She loved having it, but never felt like she deserved it. So she was forever trying to live up to the image she thought people had, was always trying to show she was one of *them*, whoever *they* are.

"Lavish. The party was lavish, around their big swimming pool." Rob laughed bitterly. "That pool belonged in a public park. It was huge and surrounded by boulders, cacti, ocotillo trees. There was a big fountain in the middle, lit up like the Bellagio. It looked like some kind of mirage imagined by Walt Disney—or Liberace. It was, though, exactly like Amber, that was Heather's mom's name: plastic, pretty, but not real.

"There were two bartenders, maids in uniform running around with trays of canapes—shrimp, lobster, pate. Liquor of all kinds flowed freely. But of course the toast, which Amber would give, had to be with Dom

Perignon. There was live music, a band that played 80s hits, Amber's favorites. They were damn good. When they weren't playing, there was a string quartet. Seriously. It was fucked-up.

"None of Heather's friends were there. The party was all people Amber and Herb wanted to impress—local politicians, minor celebrities, neighbors that had even more money than they did."

Rob paused and swallowed. The look on his face was strained.

"I found Heather alone in her room, crying. Of course she was. How would you feel if someone else took your birthday and made it all about them? I knew Heather well enough to know that, if she had her druthers, she'd have been happy with a small family dinner or a night out with the couple of girlfriends she did have. Hell, maybe even alone with a good book. I think she was reading lots of Flannery O'Connor's stuff at that point.

"I asked her, 'What do *you* want? What would make *you* happy for your birthday?'

"She looked at me with those beautiful but red-rimmed eyes. I swear I remember her saying this. 'You're my favorite uncle. I love you so much. Can we just get out of here? Go somewhere quiet—where we can eat something that isn't fancy, that doesn't cost thirty bucks a pound?'

"I knew just the spot. 'Come on. Get out of that party dress and into a pair of jeans and a T-shirt.' She complied so quickly, she was almost a blur.

"We snuck out through the kitchen door, passing only the help, who were busy getting the cake ready, arranging fresh lilies and irises around its base. One of the ladies smiled at us as though she knew we were making our getaway.

"I was glad I'd parked in the road rather than using the valets they'd set up. We got in my car and I drove straight west—to downtown Palm Springs and Sherman's restaurant on Tahquitz."

"What kind of place is that?" Jasper asked.

"It's a Jewish deli."

"Really?" Jasper had never known Lacy to eat anything other than junk. She loved Popchips, Pop-Tarts, and Corn Pops. She thought of ketchup as a vegetable.

"Yeah, it was kind of our place. She loved their matzo ball soup and the brisket sandwich, which had latkes instead of bread."

Jasper nodded. "That's my girl."

"We had a wonderful dinner that night—just the two of us. We laughed at her mom's silicone boobs, her collagen lips, her bleached-blonde hair. Heather said she looked like a cartoon or a puppet. We talked, really talked, over root beer about Heather's dreams and aspirations. She wanted to go back to school, study history, get her law degree and work as a criminal defense attorney."

"That doesn't sound like her at all," Jasper said.

Rob put a hand to his chin for a moment. "Maybe that was Heather's last night in a way. Nothing was ever the same after we got home."

Thunder rumbled outside, and the rain intensified. Jasper shivered and curled up even closer to Rob.

"Her last night?" Jasper asked.

"Yeah. It was such a great dinner, such a great time. Intimate, you know? Sherman's is also an amazing bakery, and we had this carrot cake that was to die for. We rode home on a sugar cloud, feeling close.

"And then we got there.

"The party was over. Everyone was gone.

"Amber opened the door. She looked us up and down, mascara smeared around her eyes. Swear to God, I thought of Bette Davis in *Whatever Happened to Baby Jane?*. 'How could you?' she asked, her voice a mixture of rage and hurt. 'I went to all of this trouble, and you took her away.' She hit my chest then, hard. I stumbled back. When I looked over at Heather, I could see she was scared. And I knew, too, that she'd seen this version of her mom before: drunk, loud, outraged. She tried to edge by her to get up the stairs to her room.

"She made it about halfway up when Amber stopped her by calling up the stairs, 'Go ahead. Run and hide. It's all you're good for. You're just like your father here.' And she pointed at me. I felt even more stung, more struck, than I had when she pushed me a few minutes before.

"I warned her, 'Amber, now is not the time.'

"I think it was more my saying that than her mom actually spitting out the truth in slurred words that caused Heather to stiffen with shock. She eyed me, her lower lip quivering. 'What's she talking about?' she asked me.

"I told her, 'Nothing. Nothing at all. She's drunk. She's crazy. Go to bed. We'll talk in the morning.'

"But Amber was having none of it. As Heather stood frozen on the stairs, she called up to her, 'He's your dad, honey. You've just been too stupid to realize it all these years. He was able to get it up for a woman at least once.' She laughed bitterly. 'But he didn't want you. So he gave you to us, like a castoff. But it's time you knew. God knows you're old enough.'

"Heather stared at me. And only at me. I could see the shock on her face, the pain in her eyes, and it just about killed me. 'Is this true?' she whispered.

"I closed my eyes. My gut was churning. I always thought that, someday, the truth would come out. But not like this, never like this.

"All I could do was nod my head.

"Heather turned and rushed away." Rob grew very quiet. He rolled away from Jasper.

After a while, he said, "That night was the last time I saw her until her funeral. Days later, she up and moved to Chicago. She let us know she was safe and where she was, but there was little communication after that."

Jasper pushed on Rob's shoulder, forcing him to roll over and make eye contact. "You *never* talked to her again?" Jasper could barely get the words out. He was literally afraid he would vomit. "You didn't *try*?"

"She didn't want to hear from me, Jasper. I sent emails, texts...everything went unanswered. Her phone always went to voicemail."

Jasper sat up, feeling chilled, his stomach churning. "Why? Why didn't you come to Chicago, make her see you? It's what I would have done. I would have done whatever it took!"

"I was giving her space. It was a big shock." Now Rob sounded defensive. Jasper didn't care.

"Giving her space?" Jasper numbly repeated. "For *years*?" He thought of how betrayed she must have felt, how lied to, how hurt. How she, essentially, no longer wanted to be herself. It made sense. The trauma of this revelation turned her into Lacy—and he'd never had a clue.

The secrets! The lies. Jasper couldn't fathom Lacy's pain, the enormity of it. He, all at once, understood her despair, her withdrawal.

And why she loved him.

Jasper reached over and switched on the lamp on the bedside table. He got up and began picking up his clothes where they lay scattered in disarray on the floor.

"What are you doing?" Rob asked. "Jasper, please..."

"I'm getting dressed. I need to process this."

Rob sat up and then moved toward him.

Jasper held up a hand. "Don't. I can't. Not right now." He thought of Lacy in her bed, alone, that final night Jasper had left her alone, clueless yet again about the depths of her despair, about what she needed. He tried to tell himself that it had just been that night—a night like many others—and that made the knowledge both a comfort and a horror.

In a way, it was her father who'd truly left her alone. *No. Don't think that way.*

Even though Jasper wanted to be sympathetic, to be kind, he couldn't help feeling a kind of disgust at Rob.

"Why did you give her up?" Jasper struggled into his jeans and pulled his shirt over his head. He almost fell over getting into his shoes.

"I was a kid, Jasper. I was fooling around experimenting. By the time she was born, I knew couldn't be a dad to her. Hell, I could barely parent myself back then. My brother and Amber had been trying to have a kid, and failing, for so, so long. I was trying to do the right thing."

"But *years* went by, Rob. Years! You grew up, didn't you? I can see letting someone else raise her if you weren't ready, but why did it have to be a lie? Why couldn't you just tell her and be a part of her life as a father? None of us can have too many fathers!" Jasper thought for a moment of his own dad, his silence, his lack of attention, but also of the last time they'd spoken and how he'd said "I love you."

"It would have meant so much more to her if you could have been there!" Jasper didn't know where his fury was coming from. Well, maybe he had some idea, but he couldn't let the notion rise higher than his subconscious.

The thought came anyway, even though Jasper wanted to push it away—with force. *Neither you nor Lacy had fathers. Different stories. Same end result. No wonder we saw in each other the same thing—the walking wounded, hungering for love.*

Jasper stood now at the door. "You betrayed her. You could have done more, and you didn't." Again, he thought he could be saying the same words to his own father.

"You don't understand. Jasper, please don't go. Let's talk about this."

Jasper turned. His heart pounded. "No. *You're* the reason she died. *You're* the reason life was never enough for her, why *I* was never enough for her." Jasper drew in a great quivering breath, then spat out, "I hate you."

He stood for a moment, hand on the doorknob.

Over his shoulder, Rob's voice came to him, its tone dead.

"You're right. I hate me too. Now that we've established that, you go on and get the hell out of here. I don't need you."

And Jasper rushed from the room, leaving the door open behind him.

Chapter Sixteen

Outside, the rain was torrential, freezing. But Jasper didn't feel it. He was too caught up in his own torrent of emotions.

Drenched, he tried to outrun the rain as he headed west on Chicago Avenue to the subway. It should have been light out by now, but the rains held the sky back, keeping it dark and threatening.

Shivering, Jasper headed down the stairs off the street, glad his L pass was in his pocket. He passed through the turnstile and went down another flight of stairs, ending up at the deeply underground subway station.

It was empty. The smell of mildew was in the bone-chilling air. A rat skittered along the tracks below him. Jasper was alone in the station. He needed to take several deep, calming breaths in order to stop his whole body from trembling.

The shaking wasn't simply from being cold, but also from the trauma of the scene he'd just gone through. How could things have shifted between him and Rob so quickly? He didn't know, and he honestly didn't care. Being with Rob had been a mistake. Jasper was a fool to think anything could ever come of their dalliance. Rob was old enough to be his father! He was richer than God! Once upon a time, Jasper would have thought the latter attribute would have been a gift, an advantage, something to strive for. A man to take care of him? How cool. And in a manner to which he'd definitely *not* become accustomed? Even better.

He remembered talking to Lacy about the very same thing the night she'd passed away. He could see them in his mind's eye, sitting on their living room couch watching *The Assassination of Gianni Versace* and downing pre-going-out cosmopolitans. They were just heading out the door after the show had ended when they had a curiously prescient conversation.

"*Old Andrew Cunanan had the right idea, He just had poor, if you'll pardon the pun, execution.*"

"*Oh, you're terrible, Muriel,*" Jasper said, echoing *Toni Collette in a favorite movie of theirs,* Muriel's Wedding.

"*Seriously, though, you should see if you can't find yourself a nice sugar daddy. Someone who will get you out of this shithole—*" Lacy grinned.

"*—and into the palace I deserve?*"

"*Exactly. Why not? Do it right and you can have all your dreams come true and never have to lift a finger. You're good-looking enough, Jazz, and you know it.*"

But Jasper wasn't Andrew Cunanan, thank God. The idea of having a sugar daddy, of easy money without lifting a finger, had no merit for Jasper, especially not now. Which was odd because he'd just come closer to making that opportunity into reality than ever. Jasper's previous romances and hookups had all been young guys like himself, equally underemployed or even, in some cases, not employed at all. The nearest he'd ever come to a "rich" guy was a few weeks' relationship with a law student at Northwestern. Bradley had been studying to be an intellectual property lawyer, because, as he'd told Jasper, "They make the most cash."

He had heard Bradley moved to New York City last winter, after he'd graduated.

Jasper had never been the type to long for material things. As long as he had a roof over his head, food to eat, and a little money to go out with or buy himself a new pair of jeans at the Rack, he was happy. He realized even these simple pleasures were out of the reach of many, which is why he always stopped to give what he could when he saw a homeless man or woman on the street.

He knew what he'd always wanted was love.

A quivering breath escaped him, and tears rose to his eyes as he realized that he'd run out of a room where love, maybe, just maybe, had been a possibility.

But was it? His feelings toward Rob were now so conflicted his rational mind told him to let things go. *You told him you hated him. Those are pretty final words. He told you to get out, in no uncertain terms. Besides, what he did was unforgivable. He was the catalyst that sent Lacy on her way to death.*

Jasper sighed. He looked south and spotted the lights of an approaching train. He could feel the rumble in his feet and now hear it, growing louder, kind of like the thunder up above.

Melodramatic much? Rob had his reasons, I suppose, for doing what he did with Lacy. And maybe his intentions were good. Who am I to second-guess? I hardly know the man. And Lacy had her reasons for doing what she did, which were most likely a lot more complicated than one single factor. Sure, finding out her favorite uncle was, in reality, her dad must have been a terrible shock. And maybe that did propel her out of her adoptive parents' house. But was it really a reason to kill herself? And if it was, why wait years to do it? You could have been the reason. She was in love with you and couldn't stand the idea she could never have you. Her 'parents,' her awful mother in particular, could have pushed her to that final jumping-off point. Or there could have been a whole host of things I didn't know about that made her decide to take her own life. We can never truly know someone inside and out, can we? We all keep secrets, don't we?

Jasper's thoughts slowed as the train pulled into the station. It was still early enough that there were few riders. As he'd been thinking, only one person had even come into the Chicago Avenue station—a young girl who looked as traumatized as he felt, with raccoon eyes from her mascara. He wanted to ask her if she got them from the rain or from tears, but she boarded the next car down from him.

Jasper rode in silence, barely noticing as he passed through the Clark and Division and North and Clybourn stops.

But something seized him as they rose up out of the subway. The next stop was Fullerton, and as they headed from the subway to the elevated tracks, Jasper experienced a lightening of his spirit as the train traveled from darkness into light.

In his time underground, the rain had stopped. The sky had cleared. And the blue skies and sunshine waiting for him were a kind of miracle. He marveled at the clean, pure light beaming down.

And he thought of someone other than Rob. His mind turned to another influential male figure in his life—his father.

Dad had been the repository of all of his longings for more years than he could remember. Not in a twisted way, but in a way Jasper thought all sons must long for in a father. He'd wanted him to be there for him, more than anything else. Especially since, with his mother and siblings gone, his dad was really all he had when it came to family.

So it was a continual source of frustration and, often, late-night tears that his father remained so distant all the years of Jasper's childhood and adolescence.

Even when he came out to him, his dad was nonplussed. Not condemning, to be sure, but his vague assurances that Jasper's orientation was "okay with him" were underwhelming. Jasper recalled thinking at *that* time that he would have maybe felt more loved if his dad had registered some surprise or even disdain.

But it had been as though Jasper had informed his father that he had brown hair.

He didn't know if he wanted his dad to love him, because that was too big of an ask, too much to dare dream of.

But Jasper had wanted to be *seen*. And he did things that went against his grain to that end. His father watched a lot of sports on TV, football especially (he was a fan of the Cleveland Browns and the Pittsburgh Steelers). So Jasper tried out for pee-wee football and made the team. He was a tight end (oh, the irony!). He hated every minute of the one season he'd played but had surprised himself by actually being pretty good—nimble and quick.

His father never found the time to come to a game.

Later, he ran track in high school, which he liked much better than football.

His father never came to a meet. Jasper would have loved for him to see him win his sole mile relay.

Ah, petty shit, Jasper thought. *There were kids in your class who were abused, beaten by their parents. There were some who came home to alcoholics and drug addicts. You came home to a spotless house. And there was always food on the table. You always had clothes to keep you warm.*

How dare you ask for more?

But I needed Dad's love.

Jasper was surprised to find himself at the Loyola stop already. He was almost home. The last thought he'd had, that he needed his father's love, brought him up short.

He was a tortured man whose grief never left him. He did the best he could.

He heard the thought in his head almost as though it was spoken by a feminine voice, somewhere outside himself. He even glanced behind him.

The voice continued. *Have you ever, in all your wanting and needing to be "seen," put yourself in his shoes? Here he was, not much older than you are right now, with a young family—two little kids and a new baby on the way—and suddenly his whole world is ripped out from under his feet. His wife, those kids, both born and unborn, were murdered. Brutally. Imagine the shock. Imagine the horror.*

It's no wonder Dad was numb for years!

Stepping outside of himself for perhaps the first time in his young life, Jasper didn't see his father as a dad, but as a man. He didn't see him as someone set down on this earth solely for the coveted position of raising him, but as a human being who'd experienced more shock and suffering than most.

And when he saw his father that way, as a fellow traveler on the road of life, Jasper abruptly felt swamped with emotion for him.

He stood up as he got to the Jarvis stop. He left the train quickly with tears in his eyes.

Outside, the world looked newly washed. A light breeze stirred the budding trees along Ashland Avenue as Jasper walked north to his home on Fargo.

He did his very best with me. He bore a horrible tragedy, and still he was always there for me...as much as he could be.

When Jasper got to his own door, he was eager to go inside because he remembered his dad telling him he loved him the last time they'd talked.

The apartment was empty, and Jasper was glad. Its stillness, with the sunlight slanting in through the partially open mini blinds, seemed portentous. He looked around this home he'd shared with a troubled young woman he'd loved and thought of all the mixed connections—and how easily they could be put to rights.

Without doing anything else, he plopped down on the couch and drew his phone from his pocket. He listened to distant ringing and imagined his father in one of his natty flannel shirts and Levi's, his ever-present red baseball cap.

"Dad?" he said when his father picked up.

"You got him. What's up?" Jasper took a deep breath and then said what was on his mind. "Dad. I love you." And Jasper started to cry—big, choking sobs that went on for an embarrassing amount of time, leaving him breathless, his eyes burning.

His father waited, politely, Jasper thought, for him to finish. Then he said, "I know you do, son."

Jasper wasn't surprised when they both fell to silence. Their relationship had never been much for heart-to-heart conversations, and even though a heart-to-heart was exactly what Jasper had intended when he sat down to make the call, he realized that maybe it wasn't necessary.

Maybe just telling the other "I love you" was enough.

Of course it was.

There were a few more awkward moments before Jasper said goodbye. But he hung up feeling closer to his father than he ever had.

Chapter Seventeen

Rob stood, drenched from the chest downward. The rain had at last stopped, but he felt like a sponge that had sat too long in dirty water. He looked up at the sky and could make out patches of blue peeking through the gray swatches of clouds.

He turned back to the young police officer, who was still waiting to hear what he wanted to do.

"Sir? You need us to get you somewhere?"

Rob debated, thinking of a young man, perhaps out in this same rain, getting almost as drenched as he was. He opened his mouth again to speak, unsure of what he was about to say.

"Sir? Where were you headed?"

Somehow, Rob couldn't remember how to get his mouth working to form words. *Where am I going? The easy answer is to the airport. Back to what? An empty house? A beautiful, magazine-layout-worthy house that is lovely to behold but feels like no one lives there?*

"Sir? I really need to get going. We have another call."

Rob could hear, as though there for proof, squawking on the radio she had mounted on her shoulder. He wondered if Jasper had gotten back home again, wondered if he was thinking of him with the same intensity.

"There's nothing in life that can't be fixed with some talk—and an apology."

"Beg your pardon?" the officer said as she looked over at her partner in the blue-and-white police car.

"Never mind. Can you guys give me a ride to the North Side? Um, Rogers Park?" As he spoke the words, he noticed his Uber driver rolling away from the scene in a yellow cab.

The cop rolled her eyes. In her expression was the thought that he was a nut case, like all the other nut cases she encountered every day. "You sure? That's not the direction your Uber was headed." She sighed and didn't wait for a response. "Let me see." Her hips swayed as she sidled back to the patrol car and conferred briefly with her partner, a heavy-set guy with a buzz cut.

When she came back, she said, "We need to head out. Sorry, but I can't transport you. You can call a cab."

"But I can't," Rob protested. He pulled his iPhone from his pocket. It dripped. Even though he didn't need to, he pointed to it, pronouncing it "dead."

"Okay." She blew out a long rush of air. She returned to the cruiser, got inside, and left the passenger door open as she used the car's radio, he guessed, to make a call.

She came back and told him a cab would be there in a minute or two. "Good luck," she wished him.

"I'm gonna need it."

As the news van backed out, along with the fire truck, a cab pulled in. He tapped on his horn.

The cabbie's grimace was plain to see as Rob, dripping wet, climbed into the back seat.

The driver, a Middle Eastern man in his forties, Rob guessed, continued to eye him in the rearview mirror. "Where to, sir?"

What street did Jasper live on? He drew a blank. It was on the Far North Side of the city, up by Evanston. He thought for a moment and nothing came to him, then suddenly, the name of the L stop nearby popped into his head. "Jarvis."

"Do you have an address, sir? Jarvis runs a long way west."

"Just drop me off at the L station."

The driver narrowed his eyes at him. "Really?" He probably wondered why Rob wanted to take a cab to an L station far out of the way.

But satisfying the cabbie's curiosity was not his problem. He was the paying customer, so he said simply, "Really. Now can we please go?"

As they were backing up, the sun emerged, brilliant, dousing everything with sudden golden light. The driver turned around and started up a four-lane city street. The pavement steamed. And even the litter, cracked pavement, and boarded-up storefronts looked clean. Wonderful.

Rob smiled. Hope danced in his mind, taunting, assuring.

"Thanks," Rob mumbled when they finally arrived at the L station. He reached over the seat to hand the driver a couple of twenties, but the cabbie waved them away. "It's taken care of."

Rob was confused. He shrugged. Perhaps the police had told him not to charge for the ride? Whatever the reason, he took it as an omen. "Take it anyway. I appreciate you getting me here so quickly."

He didn't know if that was true. The driver treated their ride north as though he was a driver in a race, whizzing in and out of lanes, careening through intersections where the light was changing from yellow to red, and narrowly avoiding pedestrians who dared step in his path.

Perhaps the real omen was that he'd made it here alive.

He got out of the cab and stood on the sidewalk, watching as it made its way eastbound. He knew it was east because he could see Lake Michigan from where he stood. It was only a few blocks away, and unlike its gray color earlier, it now shimmered Caribbean blue in the sunlight.

Not perfectly confident he was going in the right direction, he headed north on Ashland Avenue.

He recognized Jasper's redbrick building just past the L tracks as soon as he saw it.

He paused outside the building, wondering if this was a fool's errand, if he were just a dirty old man chasing after a boy.

It's a little late to be having second thoughts now. You told the driver to bring you here for a reason. What that reason was fueled by might bear further contemplation, but what's true is you have hope. There, just a few steps away, is a chance of something better. Don't be an idiot. Ring his buzzer. Try to make things right.

You never made enough effort with your daughter. Don't continue making the same mistake. Reach out. You might lose, but you won't know unless you try.

Rob stepped onto the stoop outside the front door and pressed the buzzer button with Jasper's name next to it.

His heart pounded. His mouth was dry.

He smiled anyway.

Chapter Eighteen

The sound of the buzzer caused Jasper to jump and wake up.

He'd dozed off on the couch after talking to his dad. He'd been in the middle of a dream, something about being in a garden with Lacy and his father, planting tomatoes. The only image he could retrieve from the dream was of the three of them squatting in the dirt. His father told them, "A little water and sunshine is all it takes."

He wiped drool from his chin as he stood. He glanced in the oak-framed mirror on the fireplace mantel and ran a hand through his hair, finger-combing it into place. At last, he headed for the door to the balcony, as he'd done many times before, to check who was outside. His second-floor vantage point had served him well in letting him know if he'd actually wanted to admit a trick he'd met online. He knew the practice was unkind and judgmental, but it *was* efficient. If someone wasn't right, they weren't right. Still, Jasper had to admit, if only to himself, that his behavior was cowardly and totally lacking in grace and consideration.

The sun had come out fully, and the temperature had soared upward at least ten degrees. The breeze in the trees was actually balmy. Still, there was that slight undercurrent of chill from the lake. He crossed his arms and leaned out over the edge of the balcony.

Rob. Jasper debated whether he should simply retreat quietly back into the apartment or see what he wanted. Seeing him down there made him feel like his dream state was continuing.

And maybe it was.

He'd taken one step backward when life, as it often does, made a different decision for him.

Rob looked up, shielding his eyes from the sun with his hand. Before Jasper could say a word, he shouted "Can I come up?"

Jasper sighed. He wanted to shout back down, "What for? Everything that needs to be said has already been said."

But you know that's rarely the case.

So he called, "I'll buzz you in." He padded to the box by the front door and pressed the button. He heard the distant bee's drone of the intercom below. Opening his front door, he waited. There was the front door opening, then the inner door by the mailboxes, all within the time allowed by the buzzer to unlock them. The doors slammed shut. Jasper leaned back, arms crossed over his chest, and listened as Rob ascended the creaking staircase. Because the building's basement was halfway aboveground, a common thing in Chicago, it was more like he lived on the third floor rather than the second.

He looked down at himself in his plaid flannel boxers and old, stretched-out white T-shirt, plain save for an ancient pinkish ketchup stain on the front. He contemplated running into his room to put something more decent on, then decided, in this instance, clothes didn't make the man.

He was grateful Stan was at work.

Rob came into view on the landing below him.

"Hey," Jasper said.

Rob paused there on the landing. "Hey," he said back.

Jasper laughed. "If this is going to be what our conversation is like, maybe we're both better off going our separate ways."

Rob came up a couple steps. There were four more to go. "Ouch." He ascended until he was just one step below Jasper. "Give me a chance, okay?"

"I thought I had." Jasper cocked his head, his hand still firmly on the door in case he wanted to swing it shut. *Is this really such a good idea? Maybe it's better to just leave well enough alone. This is the man who hurt Lacy, hurt her a lot.*

And, Jasper also thought, he was the same man, whether it was deliberate or not.

"I'm sorry," Jasper finally said. He took a step back and opened the door a little wider. Rob came in, passing in front of him, smelling of rain. He stood barely inside the apartment. Jasper couldn't help it—the man looked kind of cute because he was scared and nervous.

I can inspire him to be scared. What other powers do I have?

"You can have a seat on the couch." Because he wasn't really sure what to do with himself or what to say to Rob, he said, "I was just about to make a cup of tea. Would you like one?"

"I'd love one. Thank you." Rob sat down on the couch, back stiff, not touching the cushions. The muted buttery light lit up his face, and Jasper cursed the light for making Rob look so handsome, so tempting.

He turned, went into the kitchen, and got busy with the tea, setting the kettle to boil (after lighting the gas burner with a match), plopping a couple of PG Tips bags into chipped Human Rights Campaign mugs. He checked the pantry to see if he or Stan had any cookies and then chided himself. This wasn't that kind of visit.

What kind of visit is it, anyway?

Jasper didn't know, not for sure. Besides, the only thing close to cookies was a box of saltines, and they were stale. They'd been in there since last fall.

He could have gone into the living room and sat with Rob while waiting for the piercing scream of the kettle to alert him, but he wanted this time alone. As scared as Rob seemed of him, Jasper felt the same. There was a rat, or some other creature with tiny razor-sharp teeth, in his gut, gnawing.

After moving toward the kitchen window, he peered outside at the apartment building's backyard. The rain had left the grass damp, a little muddy. The retaining wall that held the L tracks aloft was still stained with water from the storm, looking dark here and there. An L train, one of the purple line ones that went up to Evanston, stood huffing on the tracks, almost at eye level with him. He could see figures on the train, some of them appearing to look right at him.

He suddenly remembered standing at this very window with Lacy. It was when they'd first seen the apartment and were thinking of renting it.

She peered over his shoulder. "Isn't it cool?"

"Imagine the noise," Jasper said. "We'll never sleep."

"We'll get used to it. It's so very urban, you know? I love it. And that backyard? Where else in Chicago will we find a yard that big? I mean without going way out west." She'd thought for a moment and Jasper knew an idea was percolating in her mind. "We could get a dog!" she exclaimed, as though the idea had just occurred to her.

"And you'll take care of it?"

"Why not? I take care of you."

Jasper shut his eyes and rested his forehead against the cool glass. She had. She'd always been there for him.

He knew he hadn't been there for her. Not in the way he should have been. And he wasn't thinking of being a boyfriend or anything like that. But simply to be there. He remembered his thought earlier about his dad and how he'd only wanted to be *seen*, that was all.

Lacy had wanted the same from him.

And although he loved her, he didn't know that he could say he *saw* her, really saw her. Because, if he had, maybe she'd still be here. Maybe she'd be behind him at this very moment, peering out at the day over his shoulder. Perhaps she would have made up with the man she thought was her uncle but who turned out, in a soap-opera-type twist, to be her father. She would have introduced him to Jasper and sparks would fly.

She'd be the "best man" at their wedding.

The teakettle's whistle pierced the air, made him jump. He felt yanked back down to earth.

He poured steaming water into mugs and waited a few minutes for the tea to steep. *I failed her as much as everyone else. And, like most everyone else, I didn't even know it. I didn't mean to. We're all so busy and immersed in our lives, how often do we really see each other?*

He lifted the mugs and headed toward the living room. Rob looked up at him from the couch as he set the mugs on the coffee table. "I didn't ask if you wanted cream or sugar."

"I'm sure this is fine." Rob picked up his mug.

"That's good because we don't have either. There might be some lemon juice in the fridge, though, if you like it that way."

"You mean that reconstituted stuff?"

"Yeah."

"I'll pass." Rob sipped his tea. "This is nice and strong...and that's how I like it."

Jasper sipped his own tea in silence. Tension hung in the air like old smoke, and he wasn't sure how to dissipate it. They'd said enough about tea. What was next? The weather? The current state of politics in America? Who would win *The Voice*? Jasper was about to open his mouth to comment on how bright the sun was in contrast to the storm this morning when Rob set down his mug and turned to him.

"I almost didn't make it here today."

Jasper assumed he simply meant he'd had second thoughts about seeing him again, about maybe trying to make things right between them. "Well, I'll be honest. I'm glad you did."

Rob smiled. "I am too. But I was being literal."

Jasper cocked his head. Rob spilled out his story of being swamped in his taxi and how, if he hadn't taken the split second of opportunity to get out, he might have drowned.

"It was crazy. Who would think they'd ever meet their maker *that* way?" Rob chuckled.

"Wow. That's scary." Jasper eyed him and noticed, for the first time, Rob's clothes appeared damp. "No wonder you smelled like rain when you walked in. I thought it was some fancy-schmancy cologne."

"Eau de Sewer Water?" Rob shook his head. "I know it's not a pleasant smell."

"I kind of thought it was." Jasper reached over and pressed a hand to Rob's arm, then yanked it back. "Yikes That's cold *and* wet. You want some dry stuff to change into?"

"No, I want to sit here until I get a rash from these wet clothes rubbing against my skin."

"Smartass." Jasper stood. He went into his bedroom and rummaged around in the drawers of the built-in hutch there that he'd appropriated for a dresser. He pulled out a black T-shirt and a pair of gray sweatpants. Up one drawer, he grabbed some comfy athletic socks. He returned to the living room. "Here you go." He handed the clothes to Rob.

Rob took the clothes and then eyed Jasper, frozen.

Jasper got it. Even though they'd become familiar with every nook and cranny in the other's body in the past several hours, there was now a kind of bashfulness hanging between them.

Jasper indicated the bathroom off the living room with a nod toward it. "You can shower and change in there."

When Rob came back out, Jasper cursed himself once again for feeling that queasy but delightful sensation in his gut that he recognized as lust. Sweatpants and a T-shirt could possibly be one of the sexiest and most alluring outfits a man could choose to clothe himself in—especially if he went commando. Jasper couldn't help, despite the bad friction that had passed between them, eyeing the swinging cock under the soft gray fabric. His gaze was drawn like the proverbial magnet. He forced himself to look away. He realized how easy it would be to simply sidestep their issues and fall into bed again.

Remind me again why that's a bad idea. Because you have things you need to talk about. You told the man you hated him, for one thing. He told you he had no use for you.

"Better?" Jasper asked as Rob took a seat next to him on the couch.

"Infinitely. Thank you."

They again fell to awkward silence. And it occurred to Jasper that Rob might be as averse to conflict as he was. Because Rob was older, Jasper expected him to make the first move, the first conversational gambit that may or may not lead to a reconciliation of sorts.

A reconciliation. Is that what you want?

The silence stretched out, becoming more and more awkward with each passing second. Jasper fidgeted, drank all of his tea, turned to look out the window. "It's clouding up again. Typical. Chicago is fickle." He turned back and caught Rob's gaze. "Why are you here?"

Rob's brow creased. He drew in a deep breath. "I wanted to see you. I realized that when I almost drowned. When that cop asked me where I was going, I should have said to O'Hare, which was actually where I'd been headed. But the first thought that came into my head was *you*, Jasper. Even though I probably could have gotten out of here sometime today, I couldn't leave without seeing you again." He cast his eyes down and, without looking up, asked in a soft voice, "Do you really hate me?"

"No," Jasper said immediately, because he didn't want Rob to squirm. "No, of course not. I said that in the heat of passion. And not a good passion. I wanted to blame you for Lacy's suicide, and after what you told me, it was easy to pin that on you. For a little while, it made me feel better.

"And then I figured out why. Because *I* was feeling guilty. Because *I* felt responsible." Jasper moved closer to Rob and took his chin in his hand, positioning Rob's face so that their eyes met. "I know now that you were doing your best. And so was I. Our best wasn't good enough for her, and that's sad. Really sad. If I could go back and change things, I would. God, I wish I could. But she was beyond our reach, wasn't she? And we may never know why.

"Going back in time isn't possible. We can only affect what's here. What's now." Jasper paused and in his mind's eye saw his dad, planting tomatoes. And then he saw the red tomatoes on the vine. "For example, I talked to my dad today. I told him I loved him." Jasper sighed. "I had cried and whined all my life because he never said he loved *me*. He was always so caught up in his grief over losing my mom and sister that he missed out on the one living survivor he had right in front of him.

"But you know what? I never told *him* I loved him. Not once. I just wanted to take." Jasper shrugged. "Like any kid, I suppose. But I never thought of him as simply a person, a guy in pain who soldiered on with a little boy, doing the best he could with me even though his world had been shattered." Jasper had to stop. There was a lump the size of a baseball in his throat, and his vision had blurred. He caught his quivering breath, forced himself to calm.

Rob nodded. "I understand." His expression took on a distant cast, as though he was thinking. "I was a father too, you know? And I tried to be there for her, as much as I could, without ever coming out and letting her know the truth. I know how wrong that was—*now*." He shook his head. "What they say about hindsight is true. Wouldn't life be perfect, just peachy, if we could see that 20/20?

"But we can't. We learn as we go along." Rob drew in a breath. "When I write a book, I work with my instincts, let the characters lead me in their story. The difference there is that I can go back and clean up my mistakes.

"I like that. Maybe it's why I've been alone for so long. Maybe it's why I'm a writer instead of a doctor or an accountant." He met Jasper's eyes and he smiled, sad. "Life is all instinct. We don't get the chance to go back and fix everything so it reads like a perfect narrative, so there aren't loose ends and plot holes." He laughed. "Sometimes I think life is made up solely *of* loose ends and plot holes."

Jasper edged closer. He put his head on Rob's shoulder and closed his eyes. "We can make a difference. *Now*. That's why I called my dad today. We're still awkward as hell around each other, and who knows where things will go from here. We may never have the relationship I once dreamed of, pined for. But what we'll have is based on reality—and I can be good with that.

"But we said we love each other—and that's growth I can't even measure. We may never be great pals or even a close father and son. But you know what? That's okay. Because I made a turning point—I see him for who he is. As a man. A person. And *not* my dad. We can only love what we get, not what we wish for." Jasper cuddled closer to Rob.

"You're pretty wise for your age," Rob said.

"I don't know about that. Sometimes it seems like things take forever to get through my head. But I learn as I go."

"Me too," Rob said. He slid an arm around Jasper. "She brought us together, you know."

The mention of Lacy brought Jasper up short. Hot dampness sprang to his eyes. He turned his head toward Rob. "You really think so?"

"I'd love to say 'I know so' but the truth is, I don't. No one does. I mean, knows what happens after we die. But in my writer's mind, I like to imagine a scenario where she *did* bring us together, where she's looking down with a smile at two men who were important to her and they've found each other. I like to believe that makes her happy, even if she's somewhere else. I like to believe she sees that we learned some truth about her—and that our love and memories of her live on in our hearts. Does that sound corny? Don't answer. I really don't care if it does.

"The heart speaks the truest true we know, so I'm okay with sentimental."

Jasper snuggled closer. "And I like to believe that the two of us together and our love for her and maybe for each other comforts her."

Jasper remembered Lacy out with him at this or that bar, in Andersonville or along Halsted Street. In retrospect, looking back on those vodka- and lust-fueled nights, he could safely say that he always witnessed two warring emotions on her face. One was sadness because she knew he could never be hers, not in the way she wanted. Yes, maybe it sounded egotistical, but it was true. And he was only thinking to himself here anyway.

The other thing he saw, though, was hope. He knew she could put aside her own wants and long for him to find a special someone who would love him as much as she did.

He was grateful for that hope. It meant, of course, she wanted what was best for him. But it was also a reassurance that maybe her suicide had nothing to do with him.

"That's a nice thing to believe," Rob said.

Jasper was confused for a moment, thinking Rob had read his mind. Then he recalled what he'd said about their love.

"Do you love me?" Rob asked.

And Jasper edged away, sat up straighter. "I don't know. Not yet. But I think I could, maybe."

"You don't think I'm too old? That you're just after me because I can be a father figure, the daddy you longed for but never had?"

Jasper laughed. "You don't mince words, do you?"

"In my line of work, you learn that economy—when it comes to words—often makes for the best communication and the loveliest prose. In real life, we need to think about using fewer words and making the ones we do use more meaningful. So I'll stick my neck out here and be like your dad, but *not* your dad." He took a deep breath, and then he said, "I love you, Jasper."

Jasper felt a tingle go through him, a weird electric shock, like static electricity. He scratched his head. "I've never been in love before. I don't know how to recognize it."

Rob pulled him close. "I'm willing to wait, to see if it comes up and bites you on that beautiful ass."

"Aw. Flattery will get you everywhere. Or at least into my bed."

Rob stood. In the sweats-with-no-underwear, his erection stood out proudly. "I'll take it."

Jasper followed him into the bedroom, sniffing the scent of rain.

And in the kitchen, in that window glass? He saw a reflection of her, not looking out, but looking *in*.

She was smiling.

Epilogue

The summer day outside was gorgeous.

Jasper eyed it through the sliders out to the pool. The sky was an overturned bowl of robin's-egg blue, with no clouds at all, only the gilded orb of the sun. The pool's turquoise waters shimmered, casting ever-changing reflections on the stucco walls around it. A hummingbird fluttered above one of the ocotillo trees.

The bougainvillea above the gazebo on the south end of the backyard was in brilliant fuchsia bloom.

San Jacinto stood sentry above it all, gray, white, ochre—a mass of cathedral-like spikes into the sky that Jasper imagined as a set for a movie. Get to the top and there would be nothing on the other side but an expanse of blue as far as the eye could see, like the ocean.

Rob came up to him and laid a hand on his shoulder, sharing in the view.

"Looks nice, doesn't it?"

"Yeah, like lots of the plants around here. Pretty, but when you touch them, they make you bleed."

Rob laughed. "I need to remember that metaphor. Put it in the book."

There was always a book in the works. He knew the one Rob was working on right now was about Jasper's family. A story about the murder of innocence in a small Illinois town, how it changed the survivors' lives irrevocably. Jasper hadn't been happy with the project until he learned that Rob was going to use the instrument of fiction, of storytelling, to mete out justice. The killers would be caught. The little girl would live and grow up to give her traumatized older brother the love and support he could never get from their shell-shocked father.

Her name was Lacy.

"Ah, steal from me all you want. Someday I'll write a book that will run circles around yours."

They both laughed. Rob said, "I'd welcome the competition. I'm tired of just coming up against Stephen King."

"*Pffft*. First world problems." Jasper took a step back from the glass. "What I meant about the pretty plants with their thorns and sharp edges is that the view out there could fool a person. I mean, it looks perfectly delightful, doesn't it?"

Rob nodded.

"Like, if I had a picture of that view, I'd imagine myself sitting out there in that sun on one of the lounges with, oh, maybe a pitcher of margaritas on the table next to me. I'd be wearing a pair of striped board shorts. All tan. There'd be a little line of sweat trickling down my chest."

"Careful," Rob said. "We're veering into porn territory here."

Jasper chuckled and hit him. "Stop it. You're a dirty old man."

"And you love it."

Jasper rolled his eyes. "Anyway, my point—and I do have one—is that the day out there is deceptive. It looks all welcoming and nice. Wouldn't you love to come sit out here? Bask in the sun? Revel in the warmth? That's what it seems to be saying. But those are lies. See, I just checked my phone. The weather app. The weather app tells the truth."

Rob's laugh told Jasper he'd begun to understand where Jasper was going with this line of thought. "What's the temperature?" he asked, patient.

"Wait. For. It. Today? Why it's only one hundred and fucking twenty-four." Jasper moved deeper into the cool interior of the house, into the shadows where the wash of sunlight couldn't penetrate. He sat on a white leather and chrome Eames chair. "I couldn't sit out there for more than a few minutes. The pool water is probably close to a hundred."

Rob came in and sat opposite him. "Are you complaining? I warned you what summer was like here. We can head up to Idyllwild this afternoon. It's probably a good thirty degrees cooler."

"You know I can't."

"Oh right! Your dad."

Jasper nodded. "My dad." His father was coming out to Palm Springs to visit. It would be the first time he'd ever flown, and Jasper'd had to coax him into *not* taking the train—or, God forbid, a bus from Illinois—because the man was petrified.

Dad would arrive at Palm Springs International Airport that afternoon at 3:25. It was when the day would be at its hottest, and Jasper could imagine the look of shock on his father's face when he emerged into the open-air terminal and got hit with the sauna-like air. Sauna? More like oven. Perversely, it made him smile.

Over the past few months, he and his father had done a lot of talking on the phone. Their specialties were the weather, his father's ailments, which included recently diagnosed high blood pressure and late-onset diabetes, and, if they really wanted to go heart-to-heart, what was new and decent on Netflix.

They never discussed their relationship. Certainly never the murders that had been a land mine in their family history.

And maybe they never would. But that was okay. At least they were talking.

And, after some awkward laughs, they got into the habit of always saying "I love you" before hanging up. That alone made each call worthwhile.

And now Dad was flying all the way out to Southern California. Jasper had told him to wait until October or even November, when it would be cooler, but Dad said he liked it hot, wanted to see what this so-called dry heat felt like. Jasper wasn't convinced he knew what he was getting himself in for.

"You're all ready for him?"

"Yeah, I'm gonna give him my room. I'll take the couch." Jasper, when he'd moved out from Chicago a couple of months ago, had taken a small one-bedroom apartment in Cathedral City, the Coachella Valley town right next door to Palm Springs. It was a cute little place. Three small buildings with two apartments each, gathered around a common tiled area with a pool in the center. The whole place was hidden behind fencing covered with bougainvillea. He'd found a job as a cashier at Trader Joe's and, because he had so few expenses, was able to make ends meet—just barely.

"You know you can stay here. I wish you would."

Jasper grinned slyly. He kissed Rob. "I *always* stay here. I'm wasting the pittance I make on that apartment. And I love my little place. It's like a Spanish Barbary Lane," Jasper said, referring to the place where the characters from Armistead Maupin's Tales of the City series lived.

"Break your lease. If I've told you once... You'd have so much more here. And I'd give you your precious space."

"Sure you would."

Rob was forever trying to reel Jasper in, to get him to live with him. And while the prospect *was* tempting, Jasper was determined to make it on his own out here before he committed to anything.

He didn't want to be a gold digger. He was *not*, as many guys his age out here were, looking for a sugar daddy. He still remembered, from time to time, Lacy telling him he should go after a rich guy, inspired by the miniseries they'd watched together, *The Assassination of Gianni Versace*. He would always wonder if she'd had her real father in mind when she had this brainstorm. He'd never know.

And even though he did spend the majority of nights with Rob, he liked having a place of his own to call home. He'd never had that before. He'd grown up under his father's roof. And after that, he'd always had roommates.

Living alone, even if he didn't put it into practice all that often, gave him a feeling of freedom and independence. "Besides," he told Rob, "I don't know if Dad's ready to see me shacking up with some guy."

"Some guy?" Rob's mouth dropped open in mock dismay.

"Some guy who's close to his age to boot!"

Rob had yet to meet Jasper's dad. Jasper wasn't sure how it would go. He'd sent Dad one of Michael Blake's books, and his dad, never much of a reader, had eaten it up and gone on Amazon and bought several more.

"You don't have to buy them, Dad. I can get you whatever you want for free."

His father had responded, "Ah. I want to help support the guy. He's good. I'm no freeloader, son."

Even though Jasper knew Rob could live quite well without the royalties generated by his father's purchases, he loved him for making the effort. And yes, he could see that the apple had not fallen far from the tree when it came to taking things as opposed to earning them.

And now his dad and Rob would be together at the same table. He was afraid his father would be starstruck and wouldn't behave like normal. That he'd be shy. He was a bashful man to begin with, quiet, taken to letting others take the lead.

But at least he hadn't given Jasper any grief about his and Rob's relationship. Other fathers might have been pained or squeamish that their son was gay and involved with another man. Or, if not that, that their child was taken with someone twice his age.

Jasper looked over at Rob, who was sitting, poised, on the edge of the white leather couch. He looked deep in thought. Jasper knew why—he wanted to get back to his work. Since moving here to the desert, he'd observed that about Rob, how he could disappear into the worlds he created out of his imagination—and this time, out of Jasper's personal history.

They would move in together eventually, maybe even get married. Rob was all for it and was ready right now.

But Jasper needed time. Time to discover who he was, beyond the horny kid he'd been in Chicago. Lacy's death, meeting Rob, and all the revelations tied to those two things had changed him deeply. He embraced life more than he ever had and knew how short and precious it was, knew it in his bones.

Before he contemplated taking the big step of moving in with Rob, he wanted to see what it was like to truly make his own way. Maybe become a success in his own right. Of course, Trader Joe's would never make him rich. But he *was* studying for his real estate license. He was pretty certain that the wealth Rob had was well beyond his talents (few people ever experience the kind of lifestyle being a multiple *New York Times* bestselling author afforded), but, at the very least, he could stand on his own two feet and make his way in the world comfortably.

When the day came that they set up household together, he could at least say he was contributing. Pulling his own weight. It was important to him.

Today was special. The only two men Jasper had ever said he'd loved would meet each other. Jasper so wanted things to go well.

He stood and told Rob, "You need to get back to work."

Rob didn't need to be told twice. He was off like a shot to the casita out back that was his home office.

Jasper mumbled after him, "I need to be on my way anyway. I wanted to tidy up a bit at home and stop at Ralphs to pick up provisions."

It was okay. No offense taken by Rob's sudden departure. He'd already gotten used to throwing in his lot with a man who lived out most of his days with imaginary friends.

*

Jasper sat up on the couch. Outside, through his patio sliding glass doors, he could see the black sky, the stars, and a waxing moon that was almost full.

He stood, crept over to the bedroom door, and pressed his ear against the cheap metal. He could hear his dad snoring inside. It made him smile. He was glad Dad was comfortable.

Their first day had been memorable. Jasper had taken his dad up the Palm Springs Aerial Tramway, and the views from up there, plus the much cooler mountain air, impressed his father mightily. He was childlike in his wonder at the soaring cliffs and the stunning views of the valley, and Jasper was touched that he could give him this experience.

Jasper dressed hurriedly in the dark. He thought he could make it through the week Dad was here staying at the small apartment, but he missed sleeping next to Rob in the California king.

It was his place. The warmth of Rob's body next to Jasper's own was a comfort beyond measure. More home to him than anywhere else he'd known.

Outside, he unlocked his Trek and mounted the bicycle. Rob had offered to buy him a car, and when he'd balked at the idea of such a big gift, Rob said he would cosign for a loan and lend him money for the down payment. Jasper didn't want either.

When he bought a car—*if* he bought a car—it would be with his own money.

He set off into the warm night air, thinking that the bike served his needs just fine. Rob was only a half hour away and work about the same.

And right now, even though it was still in the nineties, the air felt delicious, almost cool. Maybe he was only imagining...

But he wasn't imagining the stars. One thing about living here in the desert that city planners got right was that they kept streetlights to a minimum, so the often-clear night skies could be admired without the imposition of "light noise" like back in Chicago. There, the city lights blocked out the stars and gave the night sky a sickly yellow hue.

Even after a few months here, Jasper still marveled at the stars and could now pick out the more obvious constellations—the Big Dipper, Little Dipper, Orion. He could now even identify the cloudy mass for what it was: the Milky Way.

As he pedaled through the silent streets of Palm Springs, he suddenly had a feeling he wasn't alone. It wasn't a creepy feeling, like someone was watching him in secret or stalking him, but the easy sensation of someone being there with him, riding alongside him. Contented and free.

He smiled as a light breeze caressed his face. To his left, San Jacinto rose up, and the single light at the top of the tramway shone out like a planetary body itself. He'd point out the light to Dad tomorrow night.

Was his midnight company Lacy? His mom? His sister? Louise?

It struck him that most of the people who'd loved him were women. He didn't know quite what to make of that. Perhaps women were just more nurturing. Maybe it was mere coincidence.

He rolled up to Rob's house and another realization hit him as he let his bike fall on the desert-landscaped front lawn's rocks—the two people who loved him most in the world now were men.

Did that matter?

Maybe their love, and not their gender, was the important thing.

He fished his house key from the pocket of his shorts and then repeated the alarm code to himself as he approached the front door. He let himself in silently, then stood in the entryway, which had a direct line of sight out to the pool. The moon shone down brightly, giving a silvery glow to everything, and in that light, he saw a coyote. It was standing near the pool, its head tilted slightly upward as though it were about to bay at the moon.

Jasper didn't move. He watched the animal nearly breathlessly. Its dark silhouette at last moved away from the water's edge and toward the fence. For a moment it paused and looked back. Jasper would swear their gazes met. And then it leaped, quite gracefully, over the privacy fence.

Jasper knew he'd wonder in the morning if the vision of the coyote was just a figment of his imagination.

He turned away and crept to the bedroom, where he hoped to slide into bed next to Rob without waking him.

He'd be a nice surprise in the morning.

About the Author

Real Men. True Love.

Rick R. Reed is an award-winning and bestselling author of more than fifty works of published fiction. He is a Lambda Literary Award finalist. *Entertainment Weekly* has described his work as "heartrending and sensitive." *Lambda Literary* has called him: "A writer that doesn't disappoint..." Find him at www.rickrreedreality.blogspot.com. Rick lives in Palm Springs, CA, with his husband, Bruce, and their fierce Chihuahua/Shiba Inu mix, Kodi.

Email: rickrreedbooks@gmail.com

Facebook: www.facebook.com/rickrreedbooks

Twitter: @rickrreed

Website: www.rickrreedreality.blogspot.com

Other NineStar books by this author

Unraveling
Sky Full of Mysteries
The Perils of Intimacy
IM
Chaser
Raining Men
Blue Umbrella Sky
Third Eye
Legally Wed

Coming Soon from Rick R. Reed

The Man from Milwaukee

HEADLINES

Dahmer appeared before you in a five o'clock edition, stubbled dumb countenance surrounded by the crispness of a white shirt with pale-blue stripes. His handsome face, multiplied by the presses, swept down upon Chicago and all of America, to the depths of the most out-of-the-way villages, in castles and cabins, revealing to the mirthless bourgeois that their daily lives are grazed by enchanting murderers, cunningly elevated to their sleep, which they will cross by some back stairway that has abetted them by not creaking. Beneath his picture burst the dawn of his crimes: details too horrific to be credible in a novel of horror: tales of cannibalism, sexual perversity, and agonizing death, all bespeaking his secret history and preparing his future glory.

Emory Hughes stared at the picture of Jeffrey Dahmer on the front page of the *Chicago Tribune*, the man in Milwaukee who had confessed to "drugging and strangling his victims, then dismembering them." The picture was grainy, showing a young man who looked timid and tired. Not someone you'd expect to be a serial killer.

Emory took in the details as the L swung around a bend: lank pale hair, looking dirty and as if someone had taken a comb to it just before the photograph was snapped, heavy eyelids, the smirk, as if Dahmer had no understanding of what was happening to him, blinded suddenly by notoriety, the stubble, at least three days old, growing on his face. Emory even noticed the way a small curl topped his shirt's white collar. The L twisted, suddenly a ride from Six Flags, and Emory almost dropped the newspaper, clutching for the metal pole to keep himself from falling. The train's dizzying pace, taking the curves too fast, made Emory's stomach churn.

Or was it the details of the story that were making the nausea in him grow and blossom? Details like how Dahmer had boiled some of his victim's skulls to preserve them...

Milwaukee Medical Examiner Jeffrey Jentzen said authorities had recovered five full skeletons from Dahmer's apartment and partial remains of six others. They'd discovered four severed heads in his kitchen Emory read that the killer had also admitted to cannibalism.

"Sick, huh?" Emory jumped at a voice behind him. A pudgy man, face florid with sweat and heat, pressed close. The bulge of the man's stomach nudged against the small of Emory's back.

Emory hugged the newspaper to his chest, wishing there was somewhere else he could go. But the L at rush hour was crowded with commuters, moist from the heat wearing identical expressions of boredom.

"Hard to believe some of the things that guy did." The man continued, undaunted by Emory's refusal to meet his eyes. "He's a queer. They all want to give the queers special privileges and act like there's nothing wrong with them. And then look what happens." The guy snorted. "Nothing wrong with them...right."

Emory wished the man would move away. The sour odor of the man's sweat mingled with cheap cologne, something like Old Spice.

Hadn't his father worn Old Spice?

Emory gripped the pole until his knuckles whitened, staring down at the newspaper he had found abandoned on a seat at the Belmont stop. *Maybe if he sees I'm reading, he'll shut up.* Every time the man spoke, his accent broad and twangy, his voice nasal, Emory felt like someone was raking a metal-toothed comb across the soft pink surface of his brain.

Neighbors had complained off and on for more than a year about a putrid stench from Dahmer's apartment. He told them his refrigerator was broken and meat in it had spoiled. Others reported hearing hand and power saws buzzing in the apartment at odd hours.

"Yeah, this guy Dahmer... You hear what he did to some of these guys?"

Emory turned at last. He was trembling, and the muscles in his jaws clenched and unclenched. He knew his voice was coming out high, and that because of this, the man might think *he* was queer, but he had to make him stop.

"Listen, sir, I really have no use for your opinions. I ask you now, very sincerely, to let me be so that I might finish reading my newspaper."

The guy sucked in some air. "Yeah, sure," he mumbled.

Emory looked down once more at the picture of Dahmer, trying to delve into the dots that made up the serial killer's eyes. Perhaps somewhere in the dark orbs, he could find evidence of madness. Perhaps somehow, the pixels would coalesce, to explain, somehow, the atrocities this bland-looking young man had perpetrated, the pain and suffering he'd caused.

To what end?

"Granville next. Granville will be the next stop." The voice, garbled and cloaked in static, alerted Emory that his stop was coming up.

As the train slowed, Emory let the newspaper, never really his own, slip from his fingers. The train stopped with a lurch, and Emory looked out at the familiar green sign reading Granville. With the back of his hand, he wiped the sweat from his brow and prepared to step off the train.

Then an image assailed him: Dahmer's face, lying on the brown, grimy floor of the L, being trampled.

Emory turned back, bumping into commuters who were trying to get off the train, and stooped to snatch the newspaper up from the gritty floor.

Tenderly, he brushed dirt from Dahmer's picture and stuck the newspaper under his arm.

Also Available from NineStar Press

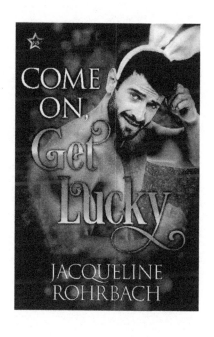

Connect with NineStar Press

Made in the USA
Monee, IL
13 January 2024

51696432R10146